TERMINAL ATROCITY ZONE

BALLARD

TERMINAL ATROCITY ZONE: BALLARD

ISBN 978-0-9857625-1-3
Edited by Candice Black
Published 2013 by The Sun Vision Press

J. G. Ballard

CRASH

A brutal, erotic novel

INTRODUCTION

BY CANDICE BLACK

The years from 1966 – which saw the publication of J.G. Ballard's early condensed fictions such as **You : Coma : Marilyn Monroe** and **The Assassination Weapon** – to 1973 – the year of the novel **Crash**, which many consider his masterwork – mark a period of intense, and often provocative literary and artistic experimentation by the author. Meshing together a variety of influences and found material – ranging from psychoanalysis, Surrealist painting and the art of insane people to "mondo" movies[1], celebrity deaths, industrial handbooks, sexological studies and texts on plastic surgery and other medical procedures – Ballard synthesised not only a new, tri-planar zone of "overheated" delinquent sexuality, but also an equally unprecedented, quasi-clinical vocabulary by which to delineate it. Reinforced by textual condensings and mutable formatting, this remains one of the most jolting and original experiments in the history of English literature.

But Ballard's experiments did not stop with literature. Always more interested in visual art – including billboard signs and advertising – and technology – in particular the phenomenon of the automobile crash – than "mere" writing, Ballard readily channeled his obsessions into a variety of artistic outlets, such as the five full-page image/text collages which form his **Advertiser's Announcements**. The author's fascination with car-crashes led to a corpus of projects removed from the printed page, most notably a 1970 exhibition of wrecked automobiles entitled "Jim Ballard: Crashed Cars", and a short film, **Crash!**, made for BBC television in 1971.

This volume, entitled "Terminal Atrocity Zone: Ballard", has been assembled in order to revisit the period of J.G. Ballard's seminal experimentation. It contains both original essays and reprinted material, the latter in the form of texts by Ballard and interviews with him. Ballard's 1969 foreword to the Danish edition of **The Atrocity Exhibition** – translated as "Grusomhedsudstillingen", it was the first version of the book to appear anywhere in the world – and his foreword to the 1974 French edition of **Crash**, both shed fresh light on the works in question. Ballard's omnivorous ideas of the period – marked by provocations such as **Alphabets Of Unreason**, a review of Hitler's *Mein Kampf* published in *New Worlds* in 1969 – are further revealed in two interviews, dating from 1970 and 1973.

Also included here are Ballard's aforementioned **Advertiser's Announcements**, plus two rarely anthologised short fictions from 1970: **Coitus 80** and **Journey Across A Crater**. **Coitus 80** – originally subtitled "A Description Of The Sexual Act In 1980" – is notable for a brief reoccurrence of Vaughan, a character first glimpsed in Ballard's short fiction **Tolerances Of The Human Face**, who would emerge fully formed in the later **Crash**. **Coitus 80** juxtaposes sexual intercourse with explicit descriptions of mammary, vaginal and penile reconstructive surgery, set to a soundtrack of traffic relentlessly crossing an overpass, thereby encapsulating the formative essence of **Crash**. **Coitus 80** is also the first in a group of short "medical" fictions based around text from plastic surgery manuals; the surgical text used here would be abbreviated and reworked by Ballard a few months later in **Mae West's Reduction Mammoplasty**, which appeared in *Ambit* 44. **Journey Across A Crater**, published a month after **Coitus 80**, continues the narrative shorthand and titled paragraph format of the fictions in **The Atrocity Exhibition**; elements such as re-enactments of road crashes, wrecked automobiles as art exhibits, "snuff" movies of crash deaths, a scarred and crippled female driver, and the erogenous zoning of car interiors all anticipate the fetishized autodromes of **Crash**.

The essays in this volume are Simon Ford's (previously published) examination of the "Crashed Cars" exhibition; Chris Horrocks' documentation of the interactions between Ballard and the artist Eduardo Paolozzi; Jack Sargeant's analysis of the film **Crash!**, plus notes on mondo movies; and Stephen Barber's overview of Ballard's condensed fictions, informed by an astute exploration of the British Library's Ballard Archive.

NOTES

1. Ballard was a great admirer of Gualtieri Jacopetti, whose controversial, genre-defining film *Mondo Cane* he reviewed in *Monthly Film Bulletin* 348 (1963). Ballard has suggested that Jacopetti's films reveal the new, fictional reality of late 20th century existence – a key idea behind **The Atrocity Exhibition**. See Jack Sargeant's "The Psychotic Screen" (page 89) for more.

BALLARD'S TERMINAL TREATMENTS

AN ESSAY BY STEPHEN BARBER

1.
TO THE INSANE

'*The Atrocity Exhibition*'s original dedication should have been "To the insane." I owe them everything.'[1]

In the mid-1960s, J.G. Ballard intensified a process, already a preoccupation of his earlier work, by which his fiction underwent condensation, narrative compacting, and insurgence into visual arts forms. That process generated a series of image/text works, the **Advertiser's Announcements**, which he published on the back-covers of issues of *Ambit* magazine between 1967 and 1971, and formed exploratory test-zones towards his most exhaustive experiment in condensed fiction, **The Atrocity Exhibition** (1970). In Ballard's short fiction, that process also involved the appropriation of pre-existent medical reports, on such subjects as interventions on sexual organs, in which Ballard restricted himself to the insertion of the names of prominent actresses and public figures, or rearranged and accentuated elements of the sparse medical narratives. In many ways, that process of experimentation with fiction, as the systematic reduction of text to its core obsessions, was undertaken through the transformation of text into image, in which text is rendered so dense, and subjected to such pressure, that it mutates into image. Image, in turn, is exacerbated to the maximal degree, with all emotional aspects rigorously excised, with the result that the narrated image abruptly oscillates from pressurised reduction to maximal, excessive expansion, and its relationship with ocular scrutiny finally disintegrates or combusts, erasing all recognisable parameters. 'This magnification of image to the point where it becomes unrecognisable is a keynote of *The Atrocity Exhibition*', as William Burroughs wrote in his introduction to the book. An insane text, with the capacity to mutate into image, is the only form able to project Ballard's wasteland-cityscapes, abandoned cinemas, motorways and mental hospitals, all populated exclusively by the terminally insane. That unsustainable strain of condensation in Ballard's writing was released by 1973 with **Crash**, but by a final aberration, it returned to his work in the notebook form of his final fiction project, **World Versus America**, from around 2005, when the contemporary world has become a global insane asylum of arbitrary reversals and compulsions, and a European coalition of America's former allies must now unite to destroy it, using terrorist strategies, as the only means to annul its irrepressible neo-colonial manias.

To condense the projection of reality to an obsessional or psychotic core always resonates with the art works and textual writings of the insane. Condensation generates an intensity and an immediacy which concurrently negate the banal and superfluous; as such, that process will also pivot at the boundary with hallucination or incoherence (like the Surrealist poetry which Ballard admired), but also instils itself with grandiosity, myth and velocity. When Ballard retrospectively assigned the dedication of **The Atrocity Exhibition** to 'the insane', for the book's 1984 RE/Search edition, he also intimated his own direction as a writer in the book's era, heading into a salutary proximity to psychotic zones (and their imageries), but stopping a moment before immersal and engulfment. All 'insane' writing and visual art is poised at that volatile precipice (otherwise, insane writers and artists would transmit only silences, voids or screams) and indicates the mutability of definitions of insanity.

In 1966, at the onset of the process of experimentation which generated the **Advertiser's Announcements**, **The Atrocity Exhibition** and **Crash**, Ballard interrogated his own aims and what his work would 'gain' through reduction and concentration: 'In *The Terminal Beach* the elements of the sequential narrative had been almost completely eliminated. It occurred to me that one could carry this to its logical conclusion, and a recent group of stories [for **The Atrocity Exhibition**] show some of the results. Apart from anything else, this new narrative technique seems to show a tremendous gain in the density of ideas and images. In fact, I regard each of them as a complete novel'.[2] The disintegration of sequence is a preoccupation that had also been pivotal to the first photographs of human figures and animals in motion. On **The Atrocity Exhibition**'s first page, Travis assembles his set of 'terminal documents' which include 'Chronograms' by the French scientist and photographer Étienne-Jules Marey; along with his English collaborator of the early 1880s, Eadweard Muybridge, Marey had instigated the process by which sequences of human movements are seized and registered through the photographic image (Muybridge, in his proto-filmic innovations, used banks of twenty or more cameras to amass multiple but separate images, while Marey deployed a single 'photographic gun' able to expose his figures near-simultaneously on the same surface, as though an image were integrally an assassination document). In order to anatomise human movement, a process of elimination necessarily took place: all continuous movements between those registered in the split-second images vanished, with the result that, in the images of Muybridge and Marey, the human body often appears subject to convulsions, facial gapings and rictus, sexually-resonant limb-spasms and oscillations – the accentuated gestural movements which fascinated Francis Bacon in his re-workings of Muybridge's images (some of which were photographic sequences of insane-asylum patients).

In his emphasis on the perceived 'tremendous gain in the density of ideas and images' to be extracted from his work on condensed fictions, Ballard evokes the contradictory proliferations that result from reduction and elimination. Much of the Surrealist art which attracted Ballard, especially the work of Max Ernst (such as *The Robing Of The Bride*, 1940, and other works whose titles are incorporated into **The Atrocity Exhibition**), possesses a dynamic of infinite proliferation, in which all space on the canvas must be excessively filled, to its maximum density. But in order to achieve that spatial excess and heighten the 'dense' mystery of figures such as those of Ernst, all conceptions of the coherent depiction of space and time must be jettisoned; Surrealist film, too, notably with Buñuel and Dalí's *Un Chien Andalou* (1929) occupies its own duration through the projection of ellipses, erasures and vanishings, often those marked with violence, upon the eye or body. Across **The Atrocity Exhibition** and Surrealist film, the fragments which remain from a process of violent elimination are saturated with a concentrational amalgam of image and text, with a distinctive ocular dynamic.

Even when his work is dedicated to the insane, and approaches their terrain, Ballard still conceives of the 'logical' process of condensation which takes him there in resolutely positive terms: his gain will be 'tremendous'. The first sentence of **The Atrocity Exhibition** evokes the exhibition of art works by the 'long-incarcerated patients' of the research-centre or insane-asylum where Travis and Nathan conduct their work. To amass or exhibit the work of the insane (and to transform that work's obsessions, into books, films or art works which inhabit a world beyond the asylum, as Ballard and innumerable others have done) possesses a lengthy history, from Hans Prinzhorn's collection of the early 1920s to large-scale 'art brut' and 'outsider art' exhibitions of the postwar and contemporary periods. Most notably, the Austrian radical psychiatrist, Leo Navratil, physically 'collected' insane artists as well as exhibiting their works, by grouping them together to live at his 'artists' house' initiative in the grounds of the vast psychiatric institution at Klosterneuberg, near Vienna, enabling that grouping of the (male) insane, whose paintings and drawings envisioned sexual compulsions and global apocalypse with the same unerring concentration as the patients of Ballard's asylum, to be exhibited together to the asylum's visitors – though each patient carried his own particular narrative (as combatants in scorched-earth conflicts such as Stalingrad, just as Ballard's figures are the ex-combatants of Vietnam, mind-destroying consumerism or car-crash duels), in a parallel way to that in which Ballard's fragments, seized at the intensively hallucinated moments between gaps of elimination, each formed, as he noted, 'a complete novel' in its own right: one proliferating to infinity.

Ballard eliminated or discarded almost all of the manuscript materials relating to **The Atrocity Exhibition**; in the archive of his work from that era, conserved after his death at the British Library in London, almost all that he allowed to survive was his own collection of the **Advertiser's Announcements**, together with a single postcard from Dealey Plaza and a short text, written in 2008, at the end of his life, in which he reflects back on the era of the book's writing and the 'overheated realm' it inhabits, focusing especially on the figure of Ronald Reagan: 'At the time, 1967, Reagan seemed a vital key to what was going wrong, both with America and the world-wide media landscapes.'[3] By 2008, the other 'key' figure in **The Atrocity Exhibition**, Ralph Nader – author of the polemical car-safety book *Unsafe At Any Speed* (1965) whose overturning precipitated **Crash**, and still a young anti-corporate activist at the time of Ballard's preoccupation with him – had himself made numerous attempts to seize the American presidency, but failed, impeded by the inability of the American population to conceive him filmically, as they effortlessly had with Reagan. The survival in Ballard's archive of his **Advertiser's Announcements**, with their particular 'density of ideas and images', intimates their seminal role in the generation of his condensed fiction, and that fiction's transmutatory infiltration into the domain of the visual image and of London's late-1960s visual arts culture. The documents' archivist, Chris Beckett, places the absence of materials relating to **The Atrocity Exhibition** within the dynamics of self-erasure projected by Ballard's archive: 'Considerably more than a brief blur, there is nonetheless a self-effacing and reductive character to Ballard's papers at the British Library: the archive is concentrated upon the successive drafts of his novels in manuscript and in typescript. Unfortunately, the draft material that has survived does not extend to Ballard's many short stories... The absence of short fiction in the archive extends to **The Atrocity Exhibition** (1970), the discontinuous narrative – or cluster of interfolded narratives – that for some critics has a greater claim than **Empire Of The Sun** to be considered Ballard's key work.'[4]

2.
BALLARD'S "ADVERTISER'S ANNOUNCEMENTS"

'Gesturing Catherine Austin into the chair beside his desk, Dr Nathan studied the elegant and mysterious advertisements which had appeared that afternoon in the pages of *Vogue* and *Paris-Match*... He rapped the magazines with his cigarette case. "These images are fragments in a terminal moraine left behind by your passage through consciousness."'[5]

Ballard's sequence of **Advertiser's Announcements** traverse art, text, and film. They form art for the globally insane; literary anti-therapies that suture unwriteable text by condensation, but simultaneously also open-up and expose the development of **The Atrocity Exhibition** into its form as a book; and double-edged 'treatments' too in a filmic sense, dually announcements (posters or billboards, like those positioned outside cinemas or on the motorways leading towards them) prefiguring impossible films that consist of only one image and are therefore the concentrated residue of an image-sequence from which all else has been eliminated, and also films that 'treat' ocular maladies – with the necessary severity of Buñuel wielding his razor at the opening of *Un Chien Andalou* – with a volatile concoction of image and text. Ballard's texts for the first, third and fourth of the five 'announcements' filmically emphasise that they are 'A J.G. BALLARD PRODUCTION', as though only the first and last movements in any creative process possess any relevance, and the advertised film-product *Homage to Claire*

Churchill had undergone a jump-cut directly from its initiatory treatment to its final 'credits' and the assignation of the film's powerful ownership, without the actual making of the superfluous film itself. Ballard's persistent highlighting in **The Atrocity Exhibition** of the figure of Abraham Zapruder, the Dallas resident who accidentally seized the instant of the Kennedy assassination in the images of his Bell & Howell 'Zoomatic' super-8 camera's Kodachrome colour celluloid frames – those isolated images (above all, frame 313, in which Kennedy's head is seen to explode) endlessly analysed and conspiratorially re-imagined, while the rest of Zapruder's extensive amateur film-oeuvre was consigned to oblivion – indicates Ballard's film-casting imperatives, and the significance of revelatory filmic residues, highlighted between eliminations or voids, in the conception of the **Advertiser's Announcements**.

In Ballard's own archive of **The Atrocity Exhibition** era, what survives are the detached covers – and in only one case, an entire copy – of the issues of the literary/arts magazine *Ambit* that published the **Advertiser's Announcements**; in most cases, Ballard has simply torn-out or scissored-away his work from the rest of the magazine's contents, so they are annulled from his archive, which is reduced to a focus on five image/text works. Ballard had worked briefly as a young man, in the early 1950s, as an advertising copyrighter, and his short stories, in particular, manifest an ongoing engagement with urban or motorway-edge billboards, hoardings, screens and posters – within which the dynamics of speed and vision are always urgently present, with the advertisement often passed-by too rapidly for any text to be assimilated by the eye (before vision shifts focus to the next instance in the sequence), so that the presence of text itself is rendered into an enigmatic blur or fragment, as with the fragments from **The Atrocity Exhibition** incorporated (in amended or expanded form) into Ballard's **Advertiser's Announcements** project. Ballard noted that, despite being an editor of *Ambit*, he had paid the magazine's commercial advertising rate (which, as its editorial information indicates, was a negligible one) for the publication of his 'announcements', had published them also in European experimental literary/arts magazines (though no trace of those further publications subsists in his archive), and had envisioned their expansive publication into global mass-media magazines such as *Vogue* and *Paris-Match*, if the advertiser's costs had not been prohibitive.

Homage to Claire Churchill, incorporating text-in-progress towards **The**

Atrocity Exhibition, appeared in *Ambit*'s issue 32 in 1967; Ballard's copy of the work is cut from the rest of the magazine, and he signed the back of the detached page in blue ink, with his surname, explicitly positioning it as an art-work whose unique status required the inscription of his signature. **The Angle Between Two Walls**, with its image-content drawn from a still from *Alone* (1963) by the London-based American experimental filmmaker Steve Dwoskin and its textual content again aligned to **The Atrocity Exhibition**, appeared in *Ambit*'s issue 33 in 1967; again, Ballard has detached his contribution from the magazine. **A Neural Interval** uses an image assigned in the work's textual elements to 'Collection: Eduardo Paolozzi' but later remembered by Ballard, in an interview with *RE/Search* journal, as being sourced from a bondage fetish-magazine.[6] The work's relationship to the development of **The Atrocity Exhibition** is explicitly highlighted by the presence in the same issue of the magazine (*Ambit* issue 36, 1968) of an entirely textual work-in-progress extract from the book; even so, Ballard has again detached his **Advertiser's Announcement** from the rest of the magazine itself. **Placental Insufficiency**, published in *Ambit* issue 45 after a break of two years, in 1970 – the year of publication of **The Atrocity Exhibition** – draws its visual element from a photograph by Les Krims, then a young and relatively little-known American photographer, and its prominent textual content (taking up a greater part of the page's surface than in the other four works, but impeded by its printing in white text on a partly white background) from **The Atrocity Exhibition**; again, in Ballard's own copy, the work is detached from the magazine. **Venus Smiles**, the final **Advertiser's Announcement**, published in *Ambit* issue 46 in 1971 and with one of its textual elements interposing the name of a car (a Ford 'Zepyhr V6') between those of the unaware subject ('Claire') and the photographer ('J.G. Ballard'), is the only one in Ballard's archive to remain attached to the entire magazine; again, its textual content is drawn from **The Atrocity Exhibition**. Each variant, prefiguration or adapted fragment from that book, across the five 'announcements', forms an autonomous art work in its own right, just as Ballard expansively conceived of the elimination-enhanced publications of work-in-progress elements of **The Atrocity Exhibition** (and other texts of that era) as 'complete' novels in themselves. For that final work, at the top-left of the page, Ballard also incorporates the binding title for his sequence of isolated works: 'Advertiser's Announcement'.[7]

Ballard originally devised the entirety of **The Atrocity Exhibition** as a large-format visual project, similar in conception to an experimental art catalogue, collaged to incorporate documentary film images and medical documents alongside the textual content, and the **Advertiser's Announcements** project forms a tangential detritus of that ambition. The art work of the classified-insane, such as that of August Walla and Henry Darger, demonstrates that no distinction can ever be made between visual and textual production; when Ballard acknowledges that he owes 'everything' to the insane, that debt encompasses the exemplar of 'logical' psychotic traversals across creative processes, along with more familiar debts to the insane such as corporeal mutation, hallucination, sexual delirium and apocalyptic obsession. Figures more dominantly associated with the production of fiction or essays who abruptly 'announced' themselves as artists, whether introducing textual elements into their art works or not, often undertook that aberrant expansion under the influence of drugs, as with Henri Michaux's mescaline-induced preoccupation with proliferating projections of the human face. Ballard's preferred Surrealist artists, such as Dalí and Hans Bellmer, were also prolific writers, or perceived no disjuncture between text and image alongside more pressing and profound disjunctures within the human body and ocular perception.

Ballard's **Advertiser's Announcements** are simultaneously low-technology and non-professional art (he had to pay for his art works to be made public, and they possess resolutely hand-made and idiosyncratic dimensions, like pages from the scrapbooks of Muybridge and Tatsumi Hijikata) and also form seminal artefacts that anatomise his preoccupations with raw sophistication, as in the exposures of Zapruder's amateur camera-work which irresistibly distilled assassination. They possess a condensed open-endedness which is also that of **The Atrocity Exhibition**, as a sequence of viral art-works that could prolong itself indefinitely (to be displayed in a book, or as a film of stilled images, like Chris Marker's 1962 *La Jeteé*, which Ballard admired, or through an undifferentiated amalgam of all media), but they are also abandoned work – Ballard's visual experiments of 1967-71, including his 'Jim Ballard: Crashed Cars' exhibition of April 1970, are terminal ones, pre-instilled with their own eradication and elimination (as a 'logical conclusion').

3.
BALLARD'S DANGERS: "WORLD VERSUS AMERICA"

'"There are dangers," he continues. "There is this deadening of the human sensibility. You go to somewhere like Kingston-on-Thames... that is very close to a modern hell. Go to the Bentall Centre" – he pronounces the name as someone might say Auschwitz-Birkenau – "and you see these huge galleries with people wandering around..."'.[8]

Ballard's 'dangers' of the final phase of his work intersect in many ways with those he had perceived in the second half of the 1960s, in the era of **The Atrocity Exhibition** and its **Advertiser's Announcements**, in proliferating American media-landscapes and their projections, and in the engulfing neo-colonial warfare epitomised by American intervention in Vietnam in the 1960s and early 70s. A number of Ballard's short stories, across the intervening decades, propose a situation in which a lengthy military or cultural conflict flares in which America and its manifestations form the 'enemy'. For Ballard, in the final years of his work, homogenising corporate consumerism constitutes a danger as malevolent as more aggressive and tangible incursions, since it annuls and deadens imagination and subversion. The history of consumerism is the history of a petrifying insanity, always the exact contrary to the active insanity to which Ballard owes 'everything'. Consumerism appears almost always American in origin for Ballard, resonating with his Shanghai childhood of vast, luxurious cars and extravagantly illustrated magazines dispatched to alien landscapes from the USA, and linked to a warfare-enhanced invasion of the European imagination. That attribution of the USA as the origin of dual invasive strategies of consumerism and neo-colonial warfare, focused on negation, formed a prominent locus of 1960s and 70s art and film (in Wim Wenders' 1976 film *Kings Of The Road,* the itinerant characters, born at the Second World War's end and now struggling to keep cinematic culture alive by repairing its last film-projectors in the warfare-created wasteland between West and East Germany, analyse how America has 'colonised our subconscious'); that meshing of consumerism and neo-colonial warfare also possesses its theoretical underpinning, in widely different idioms, in French philosophy – notably that of Jean Baudrillard, Guy Debord, and Paul Virilio – which directly impacted on Ballard's work, particularly through Baudrillard's essay "Ballard's Crash" (1976) and Ballard's own lauding of Baudrillard's *America* (1986). Ballard's last published novel, **Kingdom Come** (2006), located principally in a suburban multi-levelled atrium shopping-mall inspired by the Bentall Centre in Kingston-on-Thames – 'a town I hate', as Ballard emphasised, and dangerously close to his home in Shepperton – had interrogated those dynamics of an irresistible, ocularly-propelled consumerism, which insurges into warfare within the miniaturised zonal-city of the mall; in interviews around the book's publication, Ballard recounted his own visit to the Bentall Centre, and how his eyes and body were unwillingly meshed into the mall's spatial compulsions: 'I thought, Jesus, get out fast.'[9]

On the completion of his work on **Kingdom Come**, Ballard formulated a new project, **World Versus America**, which envisioned a more direct confrontation of his preoccupations with American military-based neo-colonial power (now, following the aerial attacks on American targets on 11 September, 2001, inextricably meshed with the disputed dynamics of terrorism) and its all-engulfing, image-driven consumerism – and also reactivated preoccupations which had been seminal to **The Atrocity Exhibition**, such as the assassination of the American President. **World Versus America** is an abandoned work, existing solely in the form of five notebooks and taken no further, and its concentrated, fragmentary formulation resonates with the condensed fictions with which Ballard had experimented in the second half of the 1960s (the British Library's cataloguing of Ballard's archive dates the notebooks to around 2005, and one possible sequence of events is that Ballard, on learning of his terminal illness, decided to pursue his final, autobiographical work, **Miracles Of Life**, 2008, in preference over **World Versus America**). Ballard intended to incorporate into the project elements drawn from television news, propaganda films, internet clips and magazine articles, in a way that recalls the collaging techniques of **The Atrocity Exhibition** and its accompanying art works; one of his formulations of the novel's narrative was that it would take the form of 'a series of testimonies'. And following on from the feature-films made of Ballard's **Empire Of The Sun** and **Crash** (both mentioned in the project's notebooks), he already explicitly envisaged **World Versus America** as a filmic project, that could even transmutate from the form of a novel into that of a film-script, and as a result, it resonates too, in its process of origination, with the filmic conception of **The Atrocity Exhibition** and its projections into the **Advertiser's Announcements**.

The weapons at Ballard's disposal for his last-ditch assault on the obliterating dynamics of America's neo-colonial and media-instilled corporate power formed slight ones: five mass-produced, spiral-bound notebooks (many pages from which have evidently been torn-out for other purposes), still adhered with stickers from 'The Card Centre, Shepperton'; four of the notebook were priced at 80p each, alongside a more luxurious, gold-coloured one, the focus of Ballard's principal work on the project, that cost 99p. Ballard's densely notational and fragmentary elements occupy only part of the notebooks' available space (in one notebook, only two pages are used, leaving the remainder of the surfaces blank). The back cover of one notebook is signed, 'JGB', as with the single signed reverse-side of one of Ballard's **Advertiser's Announcements**. All work on **World Versus America** was done by hand, mostly in blue biro with some black-biro and red-biro passages, apart from one typewritten sheet of paper which concisely summarises the project in the context of its eventual publication and, in its condensed and film-inflected form, constitutes a terminal treatment. In his essay on the Ballard archive, its curator Chris Beckett describes those materials: 'The archive includes a set of five undated notepads containing outline ideas for a novel that was not to be written, about a world war referred to as *WVA*, or *World Versus America*. Post-Iraq, a coalition of World forces has reached the end of its diplomatic patience with America's destabilising "imperial reach" and initiates global conflict by making a pre-emptive strike. Ballard summarises: "A backstory would describe the US imperial reach & attacks on other countries – its threats, use of force etc. The events that have brought a sense of despair to its last allies, & the decision to attack the US before it is too late."'[10]

In its formulation within Ballard's five notebooks, **World Versus America** presents figures, rather than characters; he evidently intended to develop a range of characters with direct involvements and commitments, to propel the novel's expansive and intricate narrative, but in the project's curtailed notebook formulation, his figures remain mysterious ciphers, unable to enter a narrative of prefigured erasure (in which America 'effectively destroys itself – a chain reaction begins'), thereby evoking the figures of Xero, Kline and Coma, poised at the peripheries of half-built or derelict motorways in **The Atrocity Exhibition**. The figure who assassinates the American President, in the envisaged book's final part, forms the 'central character', but remains hidden and disguised (for the act of assassination, he may dress as a Disneyland attendant in a Mickey Mouse costume). The targets and means for European terrorist attacks on America form far more closely delineated presences; Ballard creates lists of those targets, subdividing them into primary and 'miscellaneous' categories and using an intricate system of red-ink ticks and triple asterisks, cross-referenced across the notebooks, for such destructive means as 'suicide attacks' and 'suicide plane attacks', and to separate 'iconic' targets such as 'Hollywood Signs and Studios' from such lesser targets as 'Big Macs, Holiday Inns, etc'.

Ballard positions his narrative's terrorist war against America's maleficent neo-colonial and consumerist dangers as a deadly serious one, with satirical elements, but no element of irony; the focus of the book's planning is on the contemporary moment, but its timeframe extends backwards across seven decades, to seminal historical exemplars such as Vietnam and the Second World War. In his plan for the book and its ending, America will be approached: 'as if the country was as dangerous as Nazi Germany or the Stalinist S.U. [Soviet Union]. Not an ironic and ambiguous ending. Given that most people's feelings are broadly admiring of the US, taking it as the enemy (like a book written by a Viet Cong) would be all the more startling. An ironic ending would weaken it... Sept 11 suggests a psychological approach striking at the US's main weaknesses – its sentimentality, religiosity, adolescence...'. The end-phase of the conflict, and America's elimination, will itself form an atrocity exhibition: 'frenzied and brutal'.

Ballard also envisaged his potential reader's experience of **World Versus America** in a way that evokes (backwards and forwards across time) the emotionless but profound transits, disorders and revelations that a reading of **The Atrocity Exhibition** may precipitate. The planned novel's condensed structure would be that of: 'short chapters, almost diary-like, each seeing events from point of view of one of say 6-10 characters (it's probably not so vital here to involve reader emotionally, since the story is so strong and strange)'.[11] The curtailment of **World Versus America** itself forms a 'strong and strange' presence that intensifies its residues, and resonates too with the anti-narrational curtailments of **The Atrocity Exhibition**, on Lee Harvey Oswald's starting gun, and the **Advertiser's Announcements**, on Claire Churchill's seaweed-inscribed body, and on 'transits of touch and feeling, as serene as the movements of a dune'.

NOTES

1. Annotations, **The Atrocity Exhibition**, RE/Search, San Francisco, 1990, p.9.
2. 'Notes from Nowhere: Comments on Work in Progress', *New Worlds*, no.167, London, 1966, pp.147-51.
3. Typescript, 2008, in the J.G. Ballard collection, British Library, London.
4. Chris Beckett, 'The Progress of the Text: The Papers of J.G. Ballard at the British Library', *The Electronic British Library Journal*, London, 2011, p.8.
5. **The Atrocity Exhibition**, Panther, London, 1979, pp.58-59.
6. Interview with V. Vale, *RE/Search*, issue 8/9, San Francisco, 1984, p.147.
7. **Advertiser's Announcements**, 1967-71, in the J.G. Ballard collection, British Library, London.
8. 'The Shopping Mall Psychopath', interview by Thomas Sutcliffe, *The Independent*, London, 14 September 2000, p.7.
9. 'From Here to Dystopia', interview by Mick Brown, *The Telegraph* (magazine), London, 2 September 2006, pp.16-22.
10. Chris Beckett, 'The Progress of the Text: The Papers of J.G. Ballard at the British Library', p.15.
11. All quotations from the **World Versus America** project are from the notebooks in the J.G. Ballard collection, British Library, London. I'm grateful to Chris Beckett at the British Library for his guidance.

ADVERTISER'S ANNOUNCEMENTS

ART AND TEXT BY J.G. BALLARD

i) **HOMAGE TO CLAIRE CHURCHILL**

"Homage to Claire Churchill, Abraham Zapruder and Ralph Nader. At what point does the plane of intersection of these eyes generate a valid image of the simulated auto-disaster, the alternate deaths of Dealey Plaza and the Mekong Delta. The first of a series advertising (1) Claire Churchill; (2) The angle between two walls; (3) A neural interval; (4) The left axillary fossa of Princess Margaret; (5) The transliterated pudenda of Ralph Nader."

ii) **THE ANGLE BETWEEN TWO WALLS**

"Does the angle between two walls have a happy ending? Fiction is a branch of neurology: the scenarios of nerve and blood vessel are the written mythologies of memory and desire. Sex : Inner Space : J. G. Ballard"

iii) **A NEURAL INTERVAL**

"In her face the diagram of bones forms a geometry of murder. After Freud's exploration within the psyche it is now the outer world of reality which must be quantified and eroticised."

iv) **PLACENTAL INSUFFICIENCY**

"The X-ray plates of the growing foetus showed the absence of both placenta and umbilical cord. Was this, Dr. Nathan pondered, the true meaning of the immaculate conception – that not the mother but the child was the virgin, innocent of any of Jocasta's clutching blood. Each afternoon she would take me into the garden of the trailer park. Undressing herself, she made me memorise the trajectories of her body."

v) **VENUS SMILES**

"He worked endlessly at the photographs: left breasts, the grimaces of filling station personnel, wound areas, catalogues of Japanese erotic films. By contrast their own relationship was marked by an almost seraphic tenderness, transits of touch and feeling as serene as the movements of a dune."

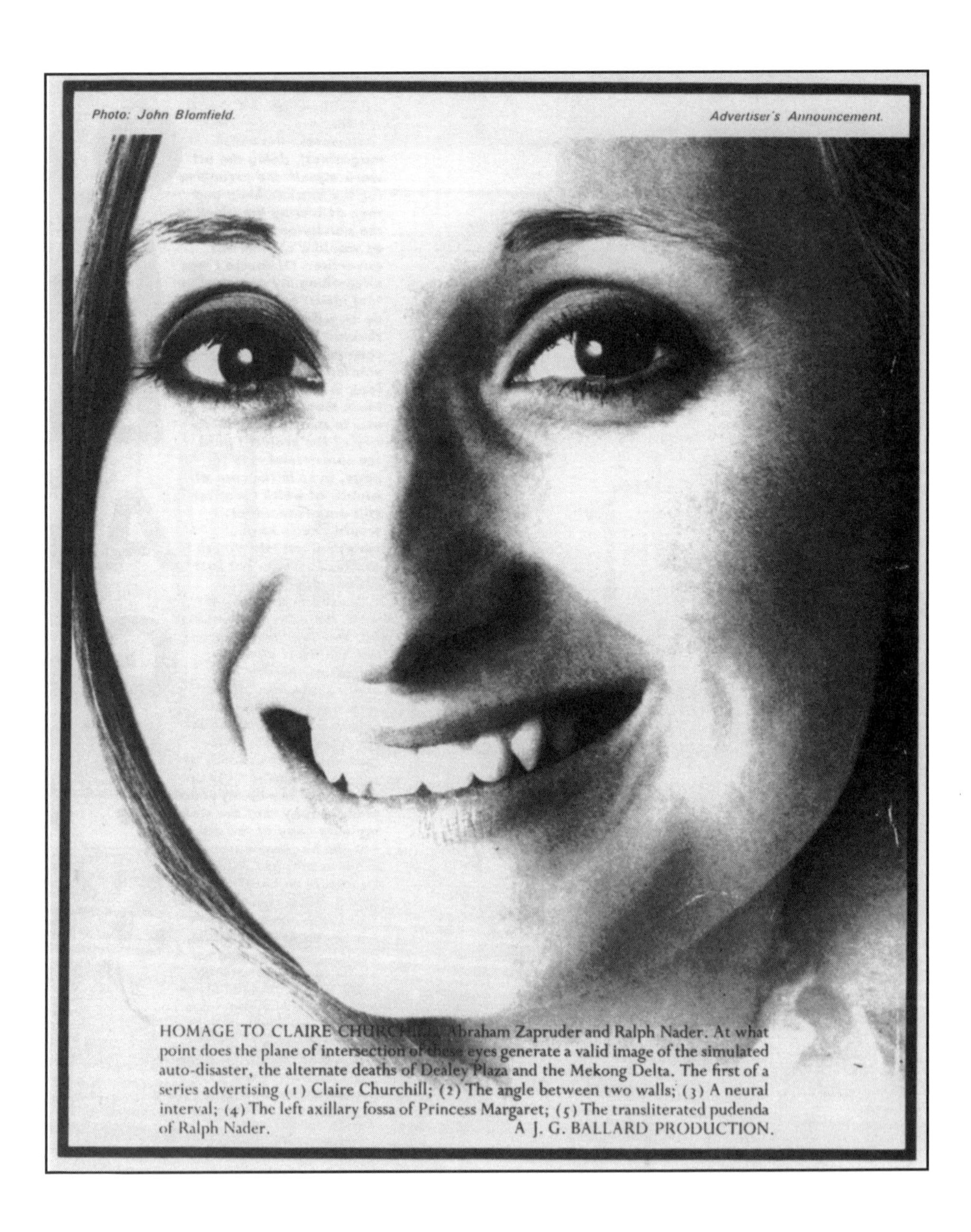
Photo: John Blomfield.
Advertiser's Announcement.
HOMAGE TO CLAIRE CHURCHILL: Abraham Zapruder and Ralph Nader. At what point does the plane of intersection of these eyes generate a valid image of the simulated auto-disaster, the alternate deaths of Dealey Plaza and the Mekong Delta. The first of a series advertising (1) Claire Churchill; (2) The angle between two walls; (3) A neural interval; (4) The left axillary fossa of Princess Margaret; (5) The transliterated pudenda of Ralph Nader.
A J. G. BALLARD PRODUCTION.

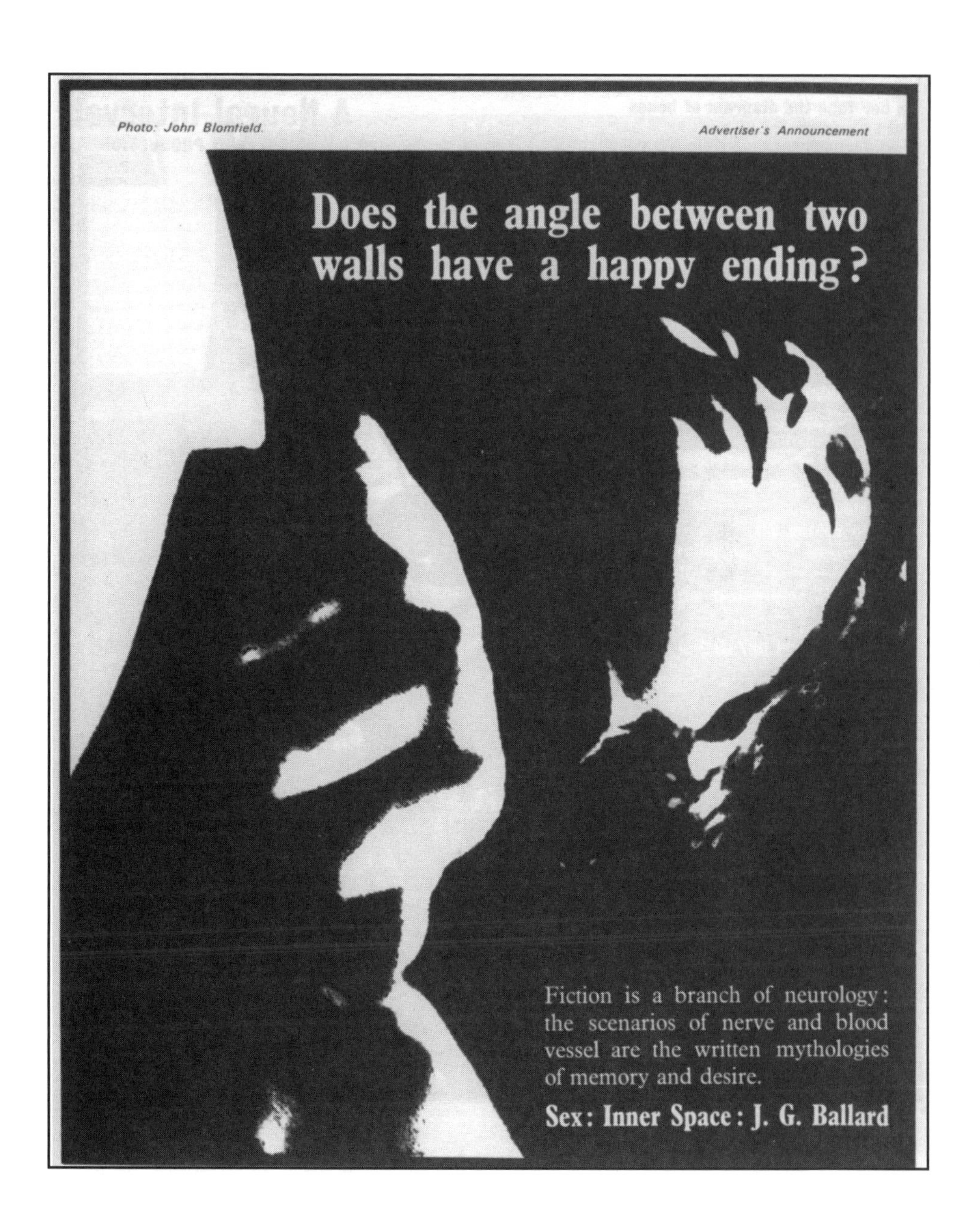
Photo: John Blomfield.
Advertiser's Announcement
Does the angle between two walls have a happy ending?
Fiction is a branch of neurology: the scenarios of nerve and blood vessel are the written mythologies of memory and desire.
Sex: Inner Space: J. G. Ballard

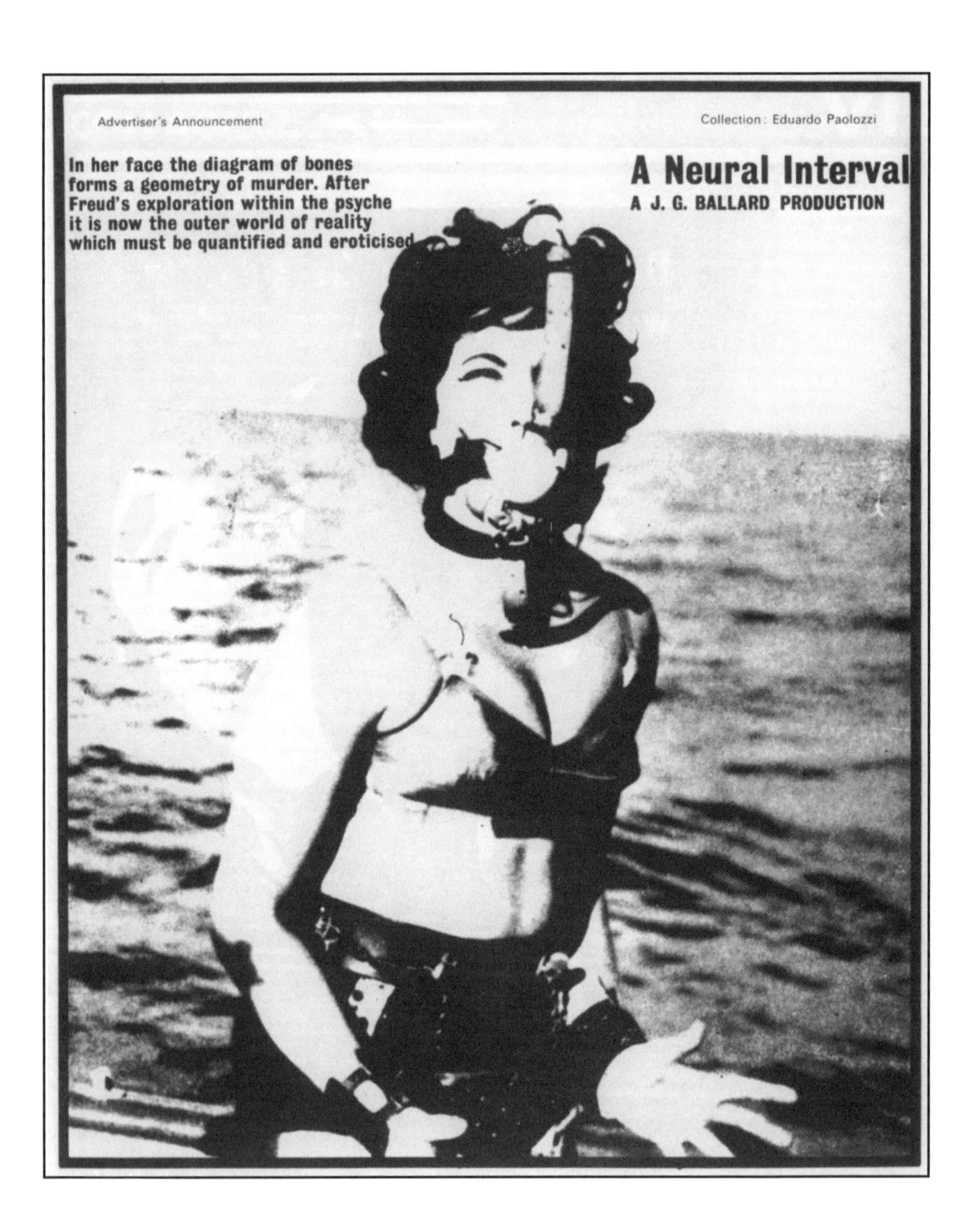
Advertiser's Announcement
Collection: Eduardo Paolozzi
In her face the diagram of bones
forms a geometry of murder. After
Freud's exploration within the psyche
it is now the outer world of reality
which must be quantified and eroticised
A Neural Interval
A J. G. BALLARD PRODUCTION

Photo: Les Krims
Advertiser's Announcement
PLACENTAL INSUFFICIENCY
The X-ray plates of the
growing foetus showed the
absence of both placenta and
umbilical cord. Was this,
Dr. Nathan pondered, the
not the mother but the child
Jocasta's clutching blood.
Each afternoon she would
take me into the garden of
the trailer park. Undressing
herself, she made me memorise the trajectories of her
body.
A J. G. BALLARD PRODUCTION

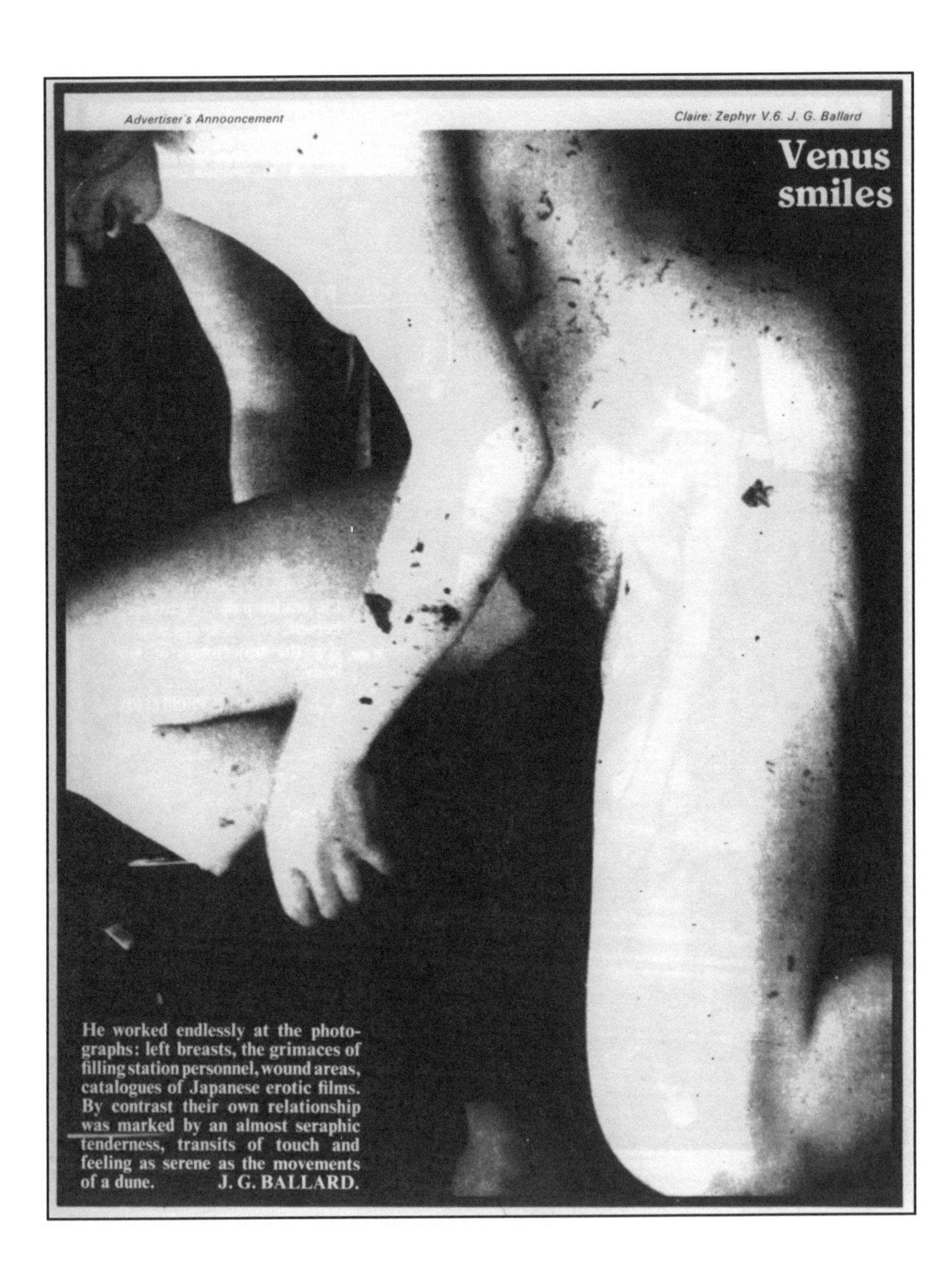
Advertiser's Announcement
Claire: Zephyr V.6. J. G. Ballard
Venus smiles
He worked endlessly at the photographs: left breasts, the grimaces of filling station personnel, wound areas, catalogues of Japanese erotic films. By contrast their own relationship was marked by an almost seraphic tenderness, transits of touch and feeling as serene as the movements of a dune. J. G. BALLARD.

FOREWORD TO "THE ATROCITY EXHIBITION"

TEXT BY J.G. BALLARD

The marriage of reason and nightmare which has dominated the 20h century has resulted in an increasingly surreal world. In the course of my own lifetime the mushroom cloud over Nagasaki has been replaced on the psychic menu by Oldenburg's giant hamburger. The murderers of presidents and cities have become media personalities, flattered by interviewers, their tics and stammers fascinating millions. The Vietnam war has been taped for television viewing. Sigmund Freud's profound pessimism in *Civilization And Its Discontents* has been replaced by McLuhan's delight in proliferating information mosaics. The hydrogen bomb is a potent symbol. Our moral right to pursue our own psychopathologies as a game is proclaimed in nearly every mass-circulation magazine, film and experimental play. The stylized violence of *Bonnie And Clyde* offers a valid iconography for department-store fashion displays. *Mondo Cane* opens an enormous market for trade in pain. The wildest fantasies of science fiction and comic-strips have become everyday realities.

The outer landscapes of our lives have become increasingly fictional, invented to serve various imaginative or conceptual ends. Only fifty years ago, to go back no further, a clear distinction existed between so-called reality – the world of commerce and industry, of our personal relations with each other – and fantasy, our dreams, hopes, ideals and so on. This relationship has now been completely reversed. The locus solus of reality exists only inside our own heads. The outer world, on the other hand, is created by advertising, by politics conducted as advertising, and is populated by characters more bizarre and incredible than any novelist could create. As for the narrow world of literature, the greatest producer of fiction is now science – the social sciences and psychology together produce an immense amount of material which belongs more to the realm of the imagination than to that of objective research. Where science once took its subject matter from nature and, for example, calculated the boiling point of a gas or the mass of a star, it now takes its raw materials from its own substance, undertaking, for instance, studies of how and where students caress each other, or how the sexual behaviour of housewives in middle-income groups is influenced by war newsreels on television or by the purchase of a new automobile.

The Atrocity Exhibition is a fiction of the 1970s. It seems to me self-evident that the next decade will move in the direction of a total transformation of all experience into fiction, whether it be the experience of our external environment or of the world inside our own heads. I believe, however, that one can distinguish between various elements in this goulash of fictions. Firstly there is the world of public events, as mediated by television, mass-circulation magazines, advertising and so on. Secondly there is the area of our own personal relationships. Thirdly there is the inner universe of our minds. These influence each other constantly. At the intersections of these three different planes lie the only points of reality we can recognize. **The Atrocity Exhibition** proposes a new geometry which allows one to perceive the elements of this three-dimensional atlas. I hope it will help the reader to navigate the deep waters of his own private experience, a voyage undertaken without the comfort of mercy.

COITUS 80

FICTION BY J.G. BALLARD

During their evenings together in the apartment

The female breast – reduction mammoplasty. The reduction in size of the female breast presents a surgical challenge of some magnitude, particularly if the nipple is to be retained as an oral mount. Many considerations should be taken into account: the age of the patient, the degree of enlargement, where the condition is one of pure hypertrophy, and finally the presence of any pathology in the breast itself. Pedicle operations are best avoided, and amputation with transposition of the nipples as free grafts is adopted as the procedure of choice. In dealing with very large breasts in younger subjects, it may be necessary to reduce the huge volumes of breast tissue in two stages. It should always be borne in mind that after the age of 30 years, breast tissue may behave in a very unfortunate manner.

Vaughan became increasingly aroused

Location of the nipple. The most important step before reduction mammoplasty is to ascertain carefully the site proposed for the new nipple. Measurements must be made in the ward before the operation with the patient sitting up. Steadying the breast with one hand, the assistant draws a line directly down to the nipple itself. The new nipple should fall on this line 7½ inches from the suprasternal notch. The nipples should be checked to ensure that they are not more than 8 inches apart. The entire skin of the chest wall is then cleaned with soap and water and wrapped in sterile towels.

by the body of the young woman.

It is possible to perform the whole operation with the knife only. An incision is carried straight down from the nipple to the sub-mammary sulcus, allowing the breast skin to be turned back as flaps. The breast should then be brought forward and laid on a board of wood. A large breast knife is carried down from above, cutting very close to the nipple. The remaining tissue of the breast is then folded round to judge whether the breast forms an acceptable shape. Care should be taken with the sutures. A suture wrongly inserted here may pull the nipple too far laterally. The skin covering is now arranged to fit snugly over the newly formed breast. The result is a roughly repaired wound from the new nipple down to the infra-mammary sulcus. It remains merely to bring the nipples out through a new hole, at the chosen position above the vertical suture line. Having found where the nipple is going to lie most comfortably and with the most desirable appearance, a circle of skin is excised. The nipple is then sutured into tis circle. The operation is a lengthy one and very often creates surgical shock.

Their acts of intercourse were marked

The sutures around the nipple are removed in 7 days. The breast must be firmly bandaged to the chest wall, using a many-tailed bandage, firm pressure being applied to the lower half of the breast. It will be some time before the breast reaches its final proportion and shape. The patient's brassiere should have a deep section and the cups should be of adequate size. Subtotal amputation with transplantation of the nipple is reserved for very large breasts. There should be no urgency about trimming scar lines or operating on the new breast until at least 6 months have passed.

by an almost seraphic tenderness,

Augmentation mammoplasty has proved extremely satisfactory in relieving the chronic anxiety caused to many women by flat or asymmetric breasts. With the patient lying on her front, two elliptical incisions are marked out on the left and right buttocks, running upward from the natal cleft. Each ellipse should be 3 inches wide and 7 to 8 inches in length. A huge wedge of skin with the underlying fat is then removed. The wound is closed in two layers; drainage is advised. The patient is then turned on her back, and the breasts are thoroughly cleaned and towellled off. An incision is made into the inframammary sulcus on each side, down to the deep fascia under the breast. The fat grafts from the buttocks are pressed into the wounds in such a way that the dermal surface faces toward the wound. The incision is then closed with interrupted sutures.

transits of touch and feeling

Finding the vagina. The more contact one has with the many types of vagina involved, the more confused one becomes. It is preferable therefore to confine oneself to the technical problems of investigating and finding a vagina, should one be present. Experience suggests that where a vagina is being sought, a laparotomy may also be necessary. With one assistant working from the abdominal cavity and the other from the rectum, each can assist the other, particularly where there is difficulty in finding a vagina that may well be absent.

as serene as the movements of a dune.

Many ingenious attempts have been made to construct a vagina with loops of intestines, or with flaps from the thigh. In general, the epithelial mould-inlay technique is the safest and most effective procedure. The essential point in the operation is to have prepared a hollow mould of perspex or vulcanite measuring 5 by 2½ inches, approximate in shape to that of an erect penis and, if possible, with a tube of reasonable width running down its entire length. The patient is placed in the lithotomy position and a thin graft is cut from one thigh, sufficient to wrap around the mould. A transverse incision is then made in the perineum and a plane reached between the bladder and rectum which is opened up until a tunnel of dimensions adequate to take the mould has been formed. The formation of the tunnel requires great care if the rectum and urethra are not be damaged. The labia minora are then incised at the introitus and sutured together across the lower end of the mould, leaving a small opening posteriorly for the escape of any discharge. Every effort must be made after the operation to see that the mould cannot be extruded.

Outside, the traffic on the flyover

The period during which the mould is retained by the patient varies a good deal with the degree of graft 'take'. With a good 'take' the graft contracture is even all around the mould and there is less tendency to extrusion. Even so, it is difficult to persuade the patient to hold on to their mould for more than 3 months. Having decided that the mould can be discarded, the union of labial tissue below the mould must be divided, the mould removed and careful cleaning of the new cavity performed. Tendency to further contracture is difficult to control. The only sure way is the physiological one of regular intercourse, and often this is felt to be tedious, undignified and ineffective by the patient. The ultimate results of this procedure with regard to sexual function are unknown.

mediated an exquisite and undying eroticism.

Penile hypospadias – before any attempt is made to perform a reconstruction on this group of cases, careful attention must be paid to the sexing of the patients. As often as not, the penis far more resembles a clitoris and, although large, it is completely hooded over and bound down. The scrotum is usually cleft and often empty. The straightening procedure must always be performed well ahead of any attempt to reconstruct the canal, and may or may not be accompanied by a meatotomy. The cosmetic result of this operation is not always perfect. There may well be an excess of tissue at the distal end of the penis resembling a wing on either side of the shaft. At least 6 months should be allowed for the patient to get over the worry about re-admission to the hospital. These wings can then be trimmed away and the organ made to look more shapely. In the experience of this surgeon, skin is never in short supply.

JOURNEY ACROSS A CRATER

FICTION BY J.G. BALLARD

Impact Zone

As he woke he felt the wet concrete cutting his face and wrists. In the drained light after the storm the causeways of a highway cloverleaf crossed the air above his head, the parapets at angles to each other like sections of ambiguous scenery. Feeling the rain-soaked fabric of his suit, he climbed the embankment. The half-built roadways formed a broken arena, the perspective model of a crater. An empty car was parked by the verge. He opened the door and sat behind the steering wheel. His hands moved across the unfamiliar instrument heads, trying to read this strange braille. As the radio blared into the damp air a young woman leaning on a balustrade fifty yards away ran back to the car. Her alert, childlike face stared at him through the windshield while he listened to the commentary. The giant fragments of the news report of a space disaster rolled across the deserted concrete.

No Entrance

As they drove along the highway Helen Clement glanced down at the man in the tattered suit slumped in the passenger seat. His heavy face, unshaven for several days, now and then turned toward the window in a bored way. His only focus of interest seemed to be the instrument console of the car – he explored its vents and toggles like an aborigine obsessed with a bright toy. Who was he – a road accident casualty, the surviving passenger of an air crash, an eccentric rapist? During the storm she had sheltered below the overpass, had seen him appear like a drowned archangel. Startled, she looked down as his strong hgand gripped her thigh.

Hell-Drivers

Through the plastic binoculars Vorster watched the last of the target vehicles burning in the centre of the stadium. As the artificial smoke rose into the evening air the crowd below began to leave. The men's faces were pinched and sallow, as if dented by the collision impacts. Vorster studied the bandaged man still sitting on the bench in the drivers' enclosure. During the climax of the show, the reconstruction of a spectacular road accident, he assumed that the man was one of the drivers masquerading as an accident casualty. But he seemed barely aware of the ugly crashes re-enacted a few yards in front of him, staring emptily across the litter of beer bottles and tyres. With a grimace, Vorster handed the binoculars to the small boy waiting impatiently behind him. He stood up and began to movea round the empty arena, wiping his damp palms on the suede leather of the camera case.

Aircrew Rescue

They walked along the airfield perimeter, avoiding the coils of barbed wire overgrown by grass. Vorster gestured at trhe shell of an abandoned helicopter. "As you can see, the runway leases expired years ago." He waited as the tall man in the shabby suit paced back to his Land-Rover. 'What sort of aircraft are you planning to bring in?" The man was staring at his reflection in the rain-streaked windshield, as if reminding himself of his own identity. The planes of his face seemed to occupy different levels, like a papier-maché pop art assemblage of a psychotic. His bloodshot eyes glanced unseeingly at Vorster. He turned away and began to scan the sky from one horizon to the other, as if marking out the landing traverses of enormous aircraft, an armada of Starlifters. Vorster leaned against the bonnet of the car, uneasily aware of the crude energy in these huge arms and shoulders. During the past hour he had deliberately spoken a meaningless jargon, but the man seemed able to make sense of his nonsense. Everything around him formed an element in a conundrum. On the centre seat lay a packet of promotional leaflets for a new airport terminal, an abstract design that looked like some unfittable piece in a Chinese puzzle. The same hemispherical module had begun to appear in a new advertisng series on the billboards along the highway.

Foramenifera

Around them the light flared through the walls of the empty aquarium tanks. Helen Clement felt his hard fingers on her elbow as he steered her through this maze of greasy glass. Since giving Vorster the slip he had become more and more preoccupied, moving between this abandoned aquarium and the hospital casualty department. Why was he buying up these arbitrary leases on derelict sites all over the city? It was almost as if he were preparing a complex of 'landing zones'. She stumbled over a coil of rubber flex, then nursed her head while he peered into the murky water in the tanks. Varying levels: fragments of a quantified womb, entry points through the foramens of memory and desire.

Nutrix Corporation

She sat in front of the dressing table, listening to the radio report of the lost space capsule. She glanced at the mirror, and involuntarily cupped her hands over her small breasts. He was staring at her body with an almost clinical detachment, as if measuring her abdomen and buttocks for yet another new perversion. All week, as they lay on the bed in this rented apartment, their acts of intercourse had become more and more abstracted. These strange perversions had at first disgusted her, but she now realised their real identity – bridges across which he hoped to make his escape. She switched off the radio when the newscast ended. Trying not to flinch, she waited as his strong hands moved across her body.

Unidentified Flying Object

As they drove along the coast road Dr Manston pointed out the sand-bars to Vorster. "The capsule was punctured during its re-entry orbit. It's just possible he escaped alive, though God only knows what happened to his mind in those last moments – you remember the reports of the Russian cosmonaut Ilyushin going insane." He stopped the car on a water-logged jetty. They stepped out and walked along the wet sand toward the pieces of debris. Dr Manston stooped to pick up a crushed mollusc. "After all, when one thinks about it, we know very little about the real effects of a disaster in space, the effects upon us, that is. One can see the disaster mimetised in terms of faulty stair angles, advertising campaigns that misfire, unsatisfactory sexual relationships, the defective arithmetic of everyday life. You said yourself that it's been a strange week in many ways. Incidentally, who is this fellow you've ben following around?"

Particle Physics

Vorster watched the paraplegics racing their wheelchairs around the basketball field. Two years earlier, while driving home one evening, he had seen Cosmos 253 breaking up on re-entry. For half a minute the sky had been filled with hundreds of glowing fragments, like an immense air force on fire. Vorster stood up as the audience cheered, and walked out among the players. The man in the shabby suit was rapidly wheeling a startled player toward the exit. What was he doing here, at a hospital for injured aircrew?

Connections, only connections

Dr Manston walked through the deserted table tennis rooms. Through the rain-streaked windows he could see the perimeter of the airfield and the beach beyond. He opened the door of the disused conservatory. The 'machine' which Vorster had described lay across a glass table, display screens around it. Dr Manston stared down at the collection of items, and then watched the solitary figure moving through the rain along the beach. He beckoned Helen Clement through the door. He waited as her nervous eyes searched the items on the table, as if hunting for the residues of misplaced affections.

Junction Makers

Dr Manston indicated the items: (1) Photograph of partly constructed motorway cloverleaf, concrete embankments exposed in transverse section, labelled 'Crater'; (2) Reproduction of Salvador Dalí's *Madonna Of Port Lligat*; (3) 500 imaginary autopsy reports of the first Boeing 747 air disaster; (4) Sequence of perspective drawings of corridors at the Belmont asylum; (5) Facial grimaces, during press conference, of Armstrong and Aldrin; (6) List of pH levels of settling beds, Metropolitan Water Board Reservoir, Staines; (7) Terminal voice-print, self-recorded, of an unidentified suicide; (8) The market analysis of a new hemispherical building-system module.

Space Platform

Dr Manston glanced sympathetically at the young woman. "Perhaps together they make up a love poem to yourself, Helen. On a more prosaic level they seem to represent the components of a strange kind of 'space vehicle' – literally, a device for moving through space in everys ense of that term: figurative, dimensional, metaphorical. A far more powerful vehicle than any astronaut's space ship." Dr Manston pointed to the solitary figure still combing the beach, his clothes drenched by the rain. An elaborate construction of drift-wood and nets had been built on the sand. "I assume that with one of those devices he plans to re-enter space."

Tracking Station

In the thin light of the hotel room she searched the drawers of the dressing table. The carpet and bedspread were covered with magazine photographs and advertising brochures, pages torn from a textbook of conical geometry. She picked up a poster advertising a new space film. His face stared out through the glassy lens of an astronaut's helmet. Had he really starred in this film, or was this just another of his strange manifestations? His personality seemed to touch everything at an oblique angle. Their own affair had been marked by the same ambiguities, the sense of his not being wholly there. Carrying the poster to the window, she looked down into the forecourt. Beyond the shadows of the sculpture garden he was pacing about on the floor of the drained swimming pool.

Equipment Failure

These equipment failures preoccupied him during this period of his search: *The drained swimming pool* – its rectilinear walls and canted floor expressed a profound disjunction of time and space, the rupture of the satellite capsule. *The breasts of Marilyn Monroe* – in the dissolving lipoids of the dead film star's breasts he saw the gradient of his own descent, his failed relationship with Helen Clement. *The dented automobile fender* – this contained the faulty geometry of his own skin areas, the unbearable asymmetry of posture and gesture.

Beckoning Glance

He waited on the kerb as the attendants helped the crippled young woman from her car into the art gallery. When they lifted the chromium trestle on to the chassis of the wheelcahir the sunlight flashed around her deformed legs. Her knowing eyes, set in a hard, pallid-skinned face, saw him staring at the junction between her thighs. Beside him, Vorster murmured in a sharp aside: "I know her – Gabrielle Saltzman, you won't..." He pushed Vorster away and followed the crippled woman into the gallery. The sunlight pressed against his skin, lying over the bright pavement like excrement.

Road Runner

All day he had been driving around the city, following the white car and kits crippled driver. At traffic intersections he stared at her toneless face, marked by a scar that smeared the right apex of her mouth across her cheek. Her powerful hands moved expertly through the gear changes. He followed her around the streets, from clinic to art gallery, watching the slightest inflection of her face. Her right-handed gear changes formed a module of exquisite eroticism.

The Drive-In Death

From the balcony of his apartment he watched the woman through the eyepiece of Vorster's cine camera. She moved across the roof garden in the chromium wheelchair. Seated by her make-up case, she would suddenly pivot and writhe, her body almost shedding its skin in a savage rictus. In particular, these activities obsessed him: *Powdering her face* – caressed by the soft puff, the talc-impacted mouth scar described the geometry of the broken car fender, the uneven transits of his affair with Helen Clement. *Urinating* – the posture of her crippled body, supported on the overhead hand-pulleys, recapitulated the grotesque perspectives of the Guggenheim Museum, the time and space of Vorster's antagonism. *Masturbating* – as he watched the extensor rictus of her deformed spine he saw again the chromium pillars of a wrap-around windshield, the reverse thrust of a taxiing Boeing.

Salon Chatter

He leaned against the crashed car mounted on its plinth in the centre of the gallery and listened to the flow of small-talk. "...a sensor on the front bumper triggers a cine camera in the dashboard binnacle, giving you a complete motion picture record of the crash injury. The crashes of the famous, by the way, might find quite a market. Ultimately, a video-tape playback will allow you to watch your own death *live*..." Gabrielle Saltzman propelled herself into the gallery, her sharp face set in a grimace of hostility. He strolled over to her with an amicable smile. Her body emanated an intense and perverse sexuality.

Vectors of Eroticism

In the garage beside the swimming pool he examined the controls of her car. Vectors of eroticism: (1) the chromium clutch treadle on the right hand quadrant of the steering wheel; (2) the black leather hand rail below the door sill; (3) the control linkages of the brake treadle mounted on the ventral surface of the steering column; (4) the imaginary treadle mounted on the dorsal surface; (5) the felted surface of the foam-plastic back support; (6) the unworn cleats of the floor-mounted clutch pedal; (7) the silver armature of the clutch treadle; (8) the worn metal runners of the chromium seat trestle; (9) the unsymmetric imprints of buttock and thigh on the foam-plastic seat; (10) the moulded lateral depression for the spinal brace; (11) the leather surgical wedge on the right hemisphere of the sea; (12) the moulded conical depression for the left thigh harness; (13) the stained leather mounting for the seat urinal; (14) the steel funnel of the urinal; (15) the cracked lucite gate of the dashboard tissue dispenser.

Mammary Gland

With Gabrielle Saltzman he studied many breasts, the time and space of nipple and areola. Together they toured the streets in her white car, analysing these breasts: of store dummies, pubertal girls, menopausal matrons, a mastectomised air hostess. The soft belly of the lower mammary curvature described the ascending flight paths of the aircraft taking off from the runways at the airfield. The skies of his mind were filled with the geometry of these rising globes. Holding the sketchbook marked with these curves, he watched Gabrielle Saltzman manoevre the car through the crowded streets with her strong hands. She confided in him with droll humour: "My own mastectomy – left breast, by the way, a difficult decision to make – was done for cosmetic reasons. Can you work that into your advertising campaign? By the way, what exactly is the product?"

Going Down

In the powdery light the parked aircraft resembled giant clinkers. On the roof of the terminal building Vorster searched the damp runways. They were strolling arm in arm like lovers through a secluded park, Gabrielle Saltzman jerking along in a nightmare hobble. Vorster rested his folder on the balcony rail. He studied the photographs. Sections of wall, wound areas, pieces of a satellite communication system, perineums, a deserted beach – elements in a weird conceptual art? Or the symbols in a new calculus of unconscious rescue? Clearly he was marooned in a world as hostile as any of Max Ernst's mineral forests.

Orbital Systems

Dr Manston gestured with the slide projector. Helen Clement sat in the passenger seat, the stub of her cigarette a wet mess between her fingers. "What these apparently obscene photographs represent are significant moments in a tragic psychodrama – for some reason pre-recorded. Miss Saltzman's role seems to be that of the crippled seductress, Madame Dalí with a club foot. One can also regard the drama as a propulsion device..." Dr Manston stepped from the car and walked to the edge of the overpass. A hundred feet below them Vorster was standing on the parapet of the embankmant, camera waiting on the rail in front of his chest.

Interlude

During this period of idyllic calm he and Gabrielle Saltzman moved together in a pleasant reverie of intimacy and warmth. In the gardens of the asylum they wandered through the patients, smiling at their empty faces as if they were servitors at a levee. As they embraced, the curved balcony of the disused terrace enclosed them like an amputated limb. The eyes of the insane watched them in intercourse.

Launch Area

He parked the heavy convertible among the dunes. The blue water of the deserted estuary moved between the concrete breakwaters like a broken mirror. The warm sunlight played on the eroded surfaces. He began to help Gabrielle Saltzman from her car. The bright chromium flashed around his fingers as they touched her wrists. As he pushed her between the clumps of sun-bleached grass he was aware of Vorster moving between the concrete embankments on the beach. The uncapped lens of the Nikon flickered in the sunlight.

Quick

His feet raced across the unset cement as he propelled the chromium chair toward the overpass. On either side the concrete pillars formed the entrances to immense vaults. At the centre of the cloverleaf, where the surrounding embankments formed a familiar arena, he stopped and let the chair spin away in front of him. It careened to one side, spilling Gabrielle Saltzman across the wet cement. He stared down at her metal body-harness as the chromium wheels revolved in the sunlight. Fifty yards away Vorster was crouched on one knee, Nikon working in his hands. He began to approach, face hidden behind the camera, feet moving in oblique passage across the concrete like the stylised dance of a deformed machine. These transits formed an enscribed graphic glass, a caption that contained Gabrielle Saltzman's scream.

K-Lines

These wounds of Gabrielle Saltzman were keys to the locked air, codes that deciphered the false perspectives of time and landscape. He looked up at the sky. At last it was open, the bland unbroken blue of his own mind. Vorster was a few paces from him, face still hidden behind the camera. The flicker of the shutter destroyed the symmetry of the landscape.

Exit Mode

Stepping across Vorster's legs, he moved away from the two bodies. On the overpass Dr Manston and Helen Clement watched from the windows of their car. He walked across the arena and entered the arcade below the overpass, at last accepting its geometry of violence and eroticism.

FOREWORD TO "CRASH"

TEXT BY J.G. BALLARD

The marriage of reason and nightmare which has dominated the 20th century has given birth to an ever more ambiguous world. Across the communications landscape move the spectres of sinister technologies and the dreams that money can buy. Thermo-nuclear weapons systems and soft-drink commercials coexist in an overlit realm ruled by advertising and pseudo-events, science and pornography. Over our lives preside the great twin leitmotifs of the 20th century – sex and paranoia. Despite McLuhan's delight in high-speed information mosaics we are still reminded of Freud's profound pessimism in *Civilisation And Its Discontents*. Voyeurism, self-disgust, the infantile basis of our dreams and longings – these diseases of the psyche have now culminated in the most terrifying casualty of the century: the death of affect.

This demise of feeling and emotion has paved the way for all our most real and tender pleasures – in the excitements of pain and mutilation; in sex as the perfect arena, like a culture-bed of sterile pus, for all the veronicas of our own perversions; in our moral freedom to pursue our own psychopathology as a game; and in our apparently limitless powers for conceptualisation – what our children have to fear is not the cars on the highways of tomorrow but our own pleasure in calculating the most elegant parameters of their deaths.

To document the uneasy pleasures of living within this glaucous paradise has more and more become the role of science fiction. I firmly believe that science fiction, far from being an unimportant minor offshoot, in fact represents the main literary tradition of the 20th century, and certainly its oldest – a tradition of imaginative response to science and technology that runs in an intact line through H.G. Wells, Aldous Huxley, the writers of modern American science fiction, to such present-day innovators as William Burroughs.

The main 'fact' of the 20th century is the concept of the unlimited possibility. This predicate of science and technology enshrines the notion of a moratorium on the past – the irrelevancy and even death of the past – and the limitless alternatives available to the present. What links the first flight of the Wright Brothers to the invention of the Pill is the social and sexual philosophy of the ejector seat.

Given this immense continent of possibility, few literatures would seem better equipped to deal with their subject matter, than science fiction. No other form of fiction has the vocabulary of ideas and images to deal with the present, let alone the future. The dominant characteristic of the modern mainstream novel is its sense of individual isolation, its mood of introspection and alienation, a state of mind always assumed to be the hallmark of the 20th century consciousness.

Far from it. On the contrary, it seems to me that this is a psychology that belongs entirely to the 19th century, part of a reaction against the massive restraints of bourgeois society, the monolithic character of Victorianism and the tyranny of the paterfamilias, secure in his financial and sexual authority. Apart from its marked retrospective bias, and its obsession with the subjective nature of experience, its real subject matter is the rationalisation of guilt and estrangement. Its elements are introspection, pessimism and sophistication. Yet if anything befits the 20th century it is optimism, the iconography of mass-merchandising, naivety and a guilt-free enjoyment of all the mind's possibilities.

The kind of imagination that now manifests itself in science fiction is not something new. Homer, Shakespeare and Milton all invented new worlds to comment on this one. The split of science fiction into a separate and somewhat disreputable genre is a recent development. It is connected with the near-disappearance of dramatic and philosophical poetry, and the slow shrinking of the traditional novel as it concerns itself more and more exclusively with the nuances of human relationships.

Among those areas neglected by the traditional novel are, above all, the dynamics of human societies (the traditional novel tends to depict society as static), and man's place in the universe. However crudely or naively, science fiction at least attempts to place a philosophical and metaphysical frame around the most important events within our lives and consciousnesses.

If I make this general defence of science fiction it is, obviously, because my own career as a writer has been involved with it for almost twenty years. From the very start, when I first turned to science fiction, I was convinced that the future was a better key to the present than the past. At the time, however, I was dissatisfied with science fiction's obsession with its two principal themes – outer space, and the far future. As much for emblematic purposes as any theoretical or programmatic ones, I christened the new terrain I wished to explore "innerspace", that psychological domain (manifest, for example, in surrealist painting) where the inner world of the mind and the outer world of reality meet and fuse.

Primarily, I wanted to write a fiction about the present day. To do this in the context of the late 1950s, in a world where the call-sign of Sputnik I could be heard on one's radio like the advance beacon of a new universe, required completely different techniques from those available to the 19th century novelist. In fact, I believe that if it were possible to scrap the whole of existing literature, and be forced to begin again without any knowledge of the past, all writers would find themselves inevitably producing something very close to science fiction.

Science and technology multiply around us. To an increasing extent they dictate the languages in which we speak and think. Either we use those languages, or we remain mute.

Yet, by an ironic paradox, modern science fiction became the first casualty of the changing world it anticipated and helped to create. The future envisaged by the science fiction of the 1940s and 1950s is already our past. Its dominant images, not merely of the first moon flights and interplanetary voyages, but of our changing social and political relationships in a world governed by technology, now resemble huge pieces of discarded stage scenery. For me, this could be seen most touchingly in the film *2001: A Space Odyssey*, which signified the end of the heroic period of modern science fiction – its lovingly imagined panoramas and costumes, its huge set pieces, reminded me of *Gone With The Wind*, a scientific pageant that became a kind of historical romance in reverse, a sealed world into which the hard light of contemporary reality was never allowed to penetrate.

Increasingly, our concepts of past, present and future are being forced to revise themselves. Just as the past itself, in social and psychological terms, became a casualty of Hiroshima and the nuclear age (almost by definition a period where we were all forced to think prospectively, I so in its turn the future is ceasing to exist, devoured by the all-voracious present. We have annexed the future into our own present, as merely one of those manifold alternatives open to us. Options multiply around us, we live in an almost infantile world where any demand, any possibility, whether for life styles, travel, sexual roles and identities, can be satisfied instantly.

In addition, I feel that the balance between fiction and reality has changed significantly in the past decade. Increasingly their roles are reversed. We live in a world ruled by fictions of every kind – mass-merchandising, advertising, politics conducted as a branch of advertising, the instant translation of science and technology into popular imagery, the increasing blurring and intermingling of identities within the realm of consumer goods, the pre-empting of any free or original imaginative response to experience by the television screen. We live inside an enormous novel. For the writer in particular it is less and less necessary for him to invent the fictional content of his novel. The fiction is already there.The writer's task is to invent the reality.

In the past we have always assumed that the external world around us has represented reality, however confusing or uncertain, and that the inner world of our minds, its dreams, hopes, ambitions, represented the realm of fantasy and the imagination. These roles, too, it seems to me, have been reversed. The most prudent and effective method of dealing with the world around us is to assume that it is a complete fiction conversely, the one small node of reality left to us is inside our own heads. Freud's classic distinction between the latent and manifest content of the dream, between the apparent and the real, now needs to be applied to the external world of so-called reality.

Given these transformations, what is the main task facing the writer? Can he, any longer, make use of the techniques and perspectives of the traditional 19th century novel, with its linear narrative, its measured chronology, its consular characters grandly inhabiting their domains within an ample time and space? Is his subject matter the sources of character and personality sunk deep in the past, the unhurried inspection of roots, the examination of themost subtle nuances of social behaviour and personal relationships? Has the writer still the moral authority to invent a self-sufficient and self-enclosed world, to preside over his characters like an examiner, knowing all the questions in advance? Can he leave out anything he prefers not to understand, including his own motives, prejudices and psychopathology?

I feel myself that the writer's role, his authority and licence to act, have changed radically. I feel that, in a sense, the writer knows nothing any longer. He has no moral stance. He offers the reader the contents of his own head, he offers a set of options and imaginative alternatives. His role is that of the scientist, whether on safari or in his laboratory faced with a completely unknown terrain or subject. All he can do is to devise various hypotheses and test them against the facts.

Crash is such a book, an extreme metaphor for an extreme situation, a kit of desperate measures only for use in an extreme crisis. If I am right, and what I have done over the past few years is to rediscover the present for myself, **Crash** takes up its position as a cataclysmic novel of the present-day in line with my previous novels of world cataclysm set in the near or immediate future – **The Drowned World**, **The Drought**, and **The Crystal World**.

Crash, of course, is not concerned with an imaginary disaster, however imminent, but with a pandemic cataclysm institutionalised in all industrial societies that kills hundreds of thousands of people each year and injures millions. Do we see, in the car crash, a sinister portent of a nightmare marriage between sex and technology? Will modern technology provide us with hitherto undreamed-of means for tapping our own psychopathologies? Is this harnessing of our innate perversity conceivably of benefit to us? Is there some deviant logic unfolding more powerful than that provided by reason?

Throughout **Crash** I have used the car not only as a sexual image, but as a total metaphor for man's life in today's society. As such the novel has a political role quite apart from its sexual content, but I would still like to think that **Crash** is the first pornographic novel based on technology. In a sense, pornography is the most political form of fiction, dealing with how we use and exploit each other, in the most urgent and ruthless way.

Needless to say, the ultimate role of **Crash** is cautionary, a warning against that brutal, erotic and overlit realm that beckons more and more persuasively to us from the margin of the technological landscape.

"CRASH!" ON TELEVISION: PRIMETIME AUTOGEDDON

AN ESSAY BY JACK SARGEANT

What follows is not concerned with any ultimate truth, neither with simply shifting through the psychosexual ruins for any singular meaning, rather it tracing a line of flight which, like the money shot – that moment of ejaculation in a porno movie – spreads into space to fertilize the imagination. The interests here are cars, speed, leather upholstery, steering wheels, crashes, injuries, trauma, bruises, suffering, discomfort and polymorphic sexuality manifested via the desire to pay witness to this copulation as chaotic fusion of flesh and technology and eroticized wounds.

A pertinent point of entry from Emile Zola's 1890 novel *La Bete Humaine*:

"She had come to look at the body... Accidents had always fascinated her. The minute she heard that an animal had been knocked down or that someone had been run over by a train she would come running to see. She had got dressed again to come to inspect the corpse."[1]

Here the swirling chaos of the Industrial Age accident emerges as a moment of spectacular, glorious eroticism, a moment in which the spectacle of the sex and death matrix becomes manifest via the twin agencies of technology and velocity. The victim: the body losing control over its parts and function, rendered utterly exposed, at the mercy of the relentless machinery, the coherent logic of the body experienced as coherent self is temporarily erased.

In the car crash, thrown against the strap of the seatbelt, wrenched and contorted, the body is victim to the vagaries of velocity and gravity, impact and resistance. Car crashes have become the moment in which, following Georges Bataille, the profane enters the world of the sacred. In the instant of the crash the car becomes the chariot which can deliver the inhabitant to the gods, and for those left behind the marks that remain, the scars of wounds and injuries, retain a hint of the sacred, the moment at which the subject briefly entered the realm of the sacred and subsequently bares its trace.

The scars and wounds of these accidents are, for some, as fascinating as the accidents themselves. A fetish than can be traced back in the case studies described in *Psychopathia Sexualis* by the pioneering sexologist Richard von Krafft-Ebing, who detailed the injury fetishists he saw:

"Case 94. Fetishism: ...Since his seventeenth year he became sexually excited at the sight of physical defects in women, especially lameness and disfigured feet... At times he could not resist the temptation to imitate their gait, which caused vehement orgasm, with lustful ejaculation....

Case 96. Fetishism: ...Since his seventh year he had for a playmate a lame girl of the same ago. At the age of twelve... the boy began spontaneously to masturbate. At that period puberty set in, and it lies beyond doubt that the first sexual emotions towards the other sex were coincident with the sight of the lame girl. Forever after only limping women excited him sexually..."[2]

In J.G. Ballard's novel **Crash** (1973) the author is explicit in his analysis of the injuries from these accidents, in his meticulous examination of back seat ejaculations, spectacular car crashes and wound fucking. Although a work of fiction, there is a parallel between the handful of individuals whose psychopathologies are detailed in the novel and the meticulous sexological case studies of Krafft-Ebing and other sexologists, a fusion of sexual arousal and injury.

Ballard's text excels in detailed descriptions of cars, crashes and sex: "scarred hands explored the worn fabric of the seat, marking in semen a cryptic diagram: some astrological sign or road intersection."[3] Later in the book Ballard describes the protagonist as he "Watched her thighs shifting against each other, the jut of her left breast under the strap of her spinal harness."[4] And finally the copulation with damaged and brutally traumatized flesh:

"I explored the scars on her thighs and arms, feeling for the wound areas under her left breast... during the next few days my orgasms took place with the scars...in these sexual apertures formed by fragmenting windshield louvers and dashboard dials in a high-speed impact..."[5]

Ballard's novel, which was famously condemned by one pre-publication reader as the work of somebody who was beyond professional help,[6] is the urtext for the transgressive fantasies associated with car crashes; traumaphilia, the sexual arousal from trauma, injuries and wounds, and symphorophilia, the arousal from orchestrating and witnessing accidents. The book follows the author's namesake as he survives a car crash and becomes immersed within a secret (but growing) community that fetishize car crashes and the resultant injuries, scars and wounds, seeking sexual satisfaction in the collisions that occur on the roads, motorways and junctions that surround Heathrow and West London. This is a work that takes meticulous pains to examine and describe the viscosity of semen, the moisture of vaginal secretions, the texture of vinyl seats and the musculature of the rectum: "still parting his buttocks, I watched my semen leak from his anus across the fluted ribbing of the vinyl upholstery".[7] Anal sex experienced through both homosexual and heterosexual liaisons recurs repeatedly in Ballard's novel. As if these simple phrases matter in this world of car crash and wound focused paraphilia, as if gender ever enters the world of the unconscious in which the specificity of the act is what defines the fetish not the gender of the object choice.

This transgressive sexual act, that negates reproduction and so fascinated the Marquis de Sade, finds a link here to the 'base,' to the annihilation of the self. Sade's detailed, meticulous sadism has been described by Gilles Deleuze in *Coldness And Cruelty* as almost mathematical, with its "repetitiveness"[8] and the multiplications of victims and sufferings, and in some way Ballard's attention to detail is similar, but in his texts the mathematics used to describe meticulous cruelty are replaced with oblique yet somehow dark references to technical detail. Ballard once had the stripper Euphoria Bliss perform a live reading of the scientific paper *The Side-Effects of Orthonovin G* in an event devised as part of an ongoing series of collaborations with *Ambit* magazine, the fusing of the supposedly antithetical elements of sexuality and science creating a surreal fetishism.

For Ballard a meticulous, forensic attention to every facet was essential:

"(1) Her ungainly transit across the passenger seat through the nearside door; (2) the conjunction of the aluminized gutter trim with the volumes of her thighs; (3) the crushing of her left breast by the door pillar, its self-extension as she swung her legs onto the sandy floor; ... (12) the jut and rake of her pubis as she moved into the driver's seat; (13) the junction of her thighs and the steering assembly; (14) the movements of her fingers across the chromium-tipped instrument heads."[9]

This attention is essential and contributes the appearance of vivid authenticity to the fantasies articulated within Ballard's writing on crashes across various texts. In **Crash** – the culmination of this work – mere action is no longer enough, details matter, from the image of Vaughan's Lincoln to the description of the flickering lights of police vehicle indicators illuminating the twin copulations associated with human coitus and the metallic penetrations of car accidents.

The nihilism of **Crash** is overwhelming, the protagonist's negation of nature and even the self, again echoes Sade, the desires are so all encompassing, they consume other and self, until all that is left is damaged flesh and ruined metal. Vaughan's ultimate desire to kill his target and himself simultaneously; a total experience that places the protagonist as analogous to Sade's sovereign man – that figure who exists beyond the simple master/slave dyad, emerging instead as an affirmation of pure, raw lived experience. Vaughan manifests as the sovereign man relentlessly pursuing his own desires knowing they will lead into the very abyss, experiencing every pleasure up to and including the supreme pleasure of annihilation.

The roots of the story of **Crash** can be found in Ballard's experimental fiction collection **The Atrocity Exhibition** (1970), which introduces the reader to an early version of Vaughan and includes numerous elements that would be expanded on in the novel that followed. Amongst shifting scenes that draw on topics such as the war in Vietnam and mondo movies, **The Atrocity Exhibition** focuses on the car crash as a moment of fetishistic concern; the book even features a fanzine for automobile accidents called *Crash* and a chapter dedicated to these interests.

"Why had he organized this exhibition of crashed cars?"[10]

In April 1970 Ballard curated a show at the New Arts Lab in London. Entitled 'Jim Ballard: Crashed Cars' this show featured three ruined cars[11] that had been dragged from wrecking yards and subsequently exhibited in the gallery. The opening night of the exhibition was marked by the presence of a topless model asking questions of the audience. Although she was meant to be nude when she saw the car wrecks she refused, as if the glimpse of her vulva or sight of her buttocks next to a ruined automobile were somehow unsuitable, destabilizing the already disturbed; confusing (or exposing) the return of the repressed manifested via the interest in copulation and annihilation. Following the evening the woman would subsequently write a scathing article in the underground magazine *Friendz*. According to Ballard the audience got rapidly drunk, bottles were broken and altercations broke out:

"There was something about those crashed cars that tripped off all kinds of latent hostility. Plus people's crazy sexuality was beginning to come out. In a way, it was exactly what I had anticipated in the book without realizing it."[12]

According to Ballard's autobiography **Miracles Of Life**, over the following month viewers responded with shocked outrage; people attacked the crashed cars, and a group of Hari Krishnas threw white paint on the cars. If Vaughan's spermatic scribblings described in the book are some primitive sigils then this religious, spiritual intervention seems to be a form of ritual cleansing, as if both driving out and calling in the forces of autopic chaos.

Little known, and barely mentioned beyond Ballard fan circles, is the short film **Crash!** made for the BBC. The film can be found archived online at sites such as YouTube, yet appears to escape the Internet Movie Data Base, while on the British Film Institute website the title is listed as *Review: Crash!* – named after the longer series it formed a part of.[13] The short work was broadcast on BBC2 at 8:30pm, two days before Valentine's Day in 1971, the screening introduced by James Mossman, the former journalist on the current affairs television series *Panorama* and series editor for the *Review* strand. Directed by Harley Cokliss (aka Cokeliss aka Cockliss),[14] the television film was made two years prior to the publication of **Crash**, instead drawing upon themes that were introduced in **The Atrocity Exhibition** and which were subsequently fully realized within **Crash**.

Made for television, the film follows Ballard as he expands on the themes that were already seducing his imagination, ideas that were emerging in his work and which would go on to inform **Crash**, as typefied by "Crash!", chapter 12 of **The Atrocity Exhibition**. The short film of the same name is primarily driven by a text by Ballard that moves, shifting from analysis of the psychology of the car to the examination of the role of the writer. Ballard's steady, calm voice-over is broken by short readings of extracts adapted from **The Atrocity Exhibition** detailing the fetishistic pleasure of the flow of women's bodies and cars. Read by an unnamed narrator, these are the case studies that inform and underpin Ballard's analysis. Accompanying these are scenes in which Ballard drives a large American car, walks around a car showroom and through a ruined car yard.

The voice-over is extra-diegetic, creating a separation between the authorial voice of Ballard from the man Ballard seen on screen; such a distance echoes the distance and separation between the author and protagonist within the book **Crash**. However, by using his own name for the novel's protagonist it becomes clear that there is an element of personal exploration that informs the book. As the author would state:

"In writing books like *Crash* or *The Atrocity Exhibition* or *High Rise*, I was exploring myself, using myself as the laboratory animal, as it were, probing around. I had to take the top off my skull when I was writing *Crash* and start touching pain and pleasure centers to see what happened."[15]

In **The Kindness Of Women** the author describes a sexual encounter in a car:

"'Jim, one day we'll be in a crash together. I'd like that... think about it now for me.' She moved diagonally across the seat and raised her thighs to expose her anus, caressing her vulva with her forefinger."[16]

This writing, this narration, this film all emerge from personal interests; the final novel **Crash** may have been fiction but the works which fed into it – the novel **The Atrocity Exhibition**, the New Art Lab display and the short film **Crash!** – escape ready classification; their taxonomy is utterly other to simple definitions.

In the film an image of a beautiful woman appears, momentarily glimpsed by Ballard. When he drives she manifests seated besides him, she appears again when he leans into a car in the showroom, her tanned hand relaxing on the plush leather interior, next to her bare legs. The light brown leather with her fingers playing on it appearing momentarily like nude flesh, as if the hand is laying between her thighs. In this instant the female flesh and the expensive interior mimic each other, and it is almost impossible to tell where one begins and the other ends. The unnamed woman is played by genre sex symbol Gabrielle Drake, an actress who in 1971 was associated with the popular science fiction series *UFO* (1969-1971) having already gained a cult reputation after appearing in episodes of television series such as *The Avengers*, *The Saint* and *The Champions*. Something of a science fiction icon, her presence here serves as an acknowledgement, perhaps even a nod, to Ballard's roots as a genre author even as the film is based on a work that would re-imagine science fiction and literature with a previously unknown velocity.

The sexuality associated with woman and car becomes paramount in the film, with slow-motion footage of the woman climbing out of and into the car, shot in tight close-ups, as her breast brushes the door, her bare legs slide under the steering wheel and so on. The narration describes the ebb and flow of her body against the unmoving car as she moves out of and into the car. It appears, through the editing of Ballard's (the character) gaze that he could be watching, a voyeur looking on, at the woman and the car. Both female and automobile are rendered here as loci of seduction.

The film moves on to a carwash, the empty car cleaned by the automatic rollers. The chrome polished, the body buffed clean. Cut to the woman in a shower, the water runs over her lips, her face, her head, her limbs, all shot in tight close-ups. The curved shapes created by the erotic contours of the female form find their mimesis within the smooth design of the vehicle, the flow of a fender and the architecture of the hood. The meticulous close-ups of the female anatomy with water pouring over it continues, rivulets from the shower flow across and down her flesh, dripping from above before pooling into splashing pools located in the folds of limbs. Until finally a pink nipple turns to face the camera, partly erect, the water flowing around the bud and down over the pale areole. Again this is cut with an image of the car. The eroticism of the vehicle is complete. While Ballard's narration has been constant throughout, this sequence is marked by the absence of the narrator, instead there is the sound of flowing water, but somewhere, quiet in the mix, there seems to be an echo, as if something more is at stake here.

The scenes shift, Ballard is walking through mounds of wrecked cars, looking upwards his eyes not facing heavenwards but instead focusing on the pillars of crushed, broken, torn and ruined automobiles that are stacked in piles three high, towering above him like memorials to the thousands of deaths inflicted on the highways of the world. The narration now shifts gear and begins to focus on the car crash as the way in which many will meet death. Then, speculating, Ballard's voice continues: "Are we just victims in a totally meaningless tragedy, or does it in fact take place with our unconscious, and even conscious, connivance?" The thought seems preposterous, but he continues, "Each year hundreds of thousands of people are killed in car crashes all over the world. Millions are injured. Are these arranged deaths arranged by the colliding forces of the technological landscape, by our own unconscious fantasies about power and aggression, our obsessions with consumer goods and desires, the overlaying fictions that are more and more taking the place of reality?" These themes would come to increasingly inform Ballard's work. "If we really feared the car crash," he says, "none of us would be able to drive a car."

As Ballard walks through the ruined landscape of burned out, viciously dented and utterly broken cars, he once more catches a glimpse of the woman. Standing still she appears as almost a mannequin rendered unmoving, transfixed as assuredly as a rabbit in the headlights of an oncoming vehicle. A series of shots establish his gaze at her. After a number of close-ups of a ruined car Ballard climbs into the crushed machine, he discusses the style of the instrument panel as the model of imminent wounds and possible annihilation: "the shape of our own death." Footage shows Drake – moments before seen in the shower, her flesh, her curves and her breast dripping with fresh water – now blood soaked and slumped over her steering wheel. The soundtrack becomes a synthesized alarm, escalating in intensity, an electronic scream. The woman lays slumped and bloodied, her head laying on the steering wheel. Blood on her bare thighs is visible beneath her short fashionable skirt. In a series of jerky animated shots the film follows her as she regains consciousness she tries to open the door, and slumps from the ruined car. The cinematic style of live action animation created from a series of photographs of the woman in the car recall experimental film and serve to emphasize the disjointed psychology of the adrenalized and shocked victim as she drags her bloodied body from the wreck. The soundtrack of electronic 'noises' escalates in intensity during these scenes creating a synthesized combination of high-pitched whines and electronic bleeps and wails.

"A film of automobile accidents... was also found to have a marked erotic content."[17]

The film cuts to Ballard driving his car, his voiceover describes his appreciation for scientific and educational films depicting slow-motion car crashes, in which cars are meticulously wrecked and their cargo of crash-test dummies exposed to the massive traumas of these staged impacts. As he speaks the footage of these experimental collisions is screened, crash after crash, cars pounding into each other, crash barriers, trees and solid walls, their once perfectly engineered forms impacted and crushed, the metal frames reduced almost instantly to bent, distorted and useless wrecks. The last of these clips – an extreme slow motion shot of a car driven into a concrete wall in a lab – takes place free of voice over, instead the sound design recalls the sound of metal rending and scraping and bending and collapsing and screaming as it is compacted by the forces of the impact. The emphasis on watching this crash, on listening to the sounds of the collapsing metal, echoes the cum-shot in a porn film. This is the moment in which the crash is finally and fully realized for the audience's gaze, a moment of secret pleasure. When Ballard's narration resumes it brings the viewers back from this as he delivers what will be his final comments.

Now in endless circulation, Ballard drives further and further around the contemporary architecture of suburban London: flyovers, motorways and multi-storey car parks, this is the Ballardian world that defined **The Atrocity Exhibition** and his seminal 70s novels **Crash** (1973), **Concrete Island** (1974) and **High Rise** (1975), an early map of the mise-en-scène of the post-industrial world. A transitory landscape that emerges as both mythical and unconscious in Ballard's work. As he drives he glances at his passenger; the woman is sitting next to him once again. A fugue figure that draws him away from himself, she appears almost like an angel of autogeddon, the symbolic figure of auto death. Finally, on the roof of a multi-storey car park he views the horizon, a limitless concrete city in which pleasures will emerge from the spaces between.

Ballard's glorious fusion of sex, injury and death in the car crash realized in this short film plays on images of blood and sex, the thick heavy blood pooling on her skirt indicative of abdominal injuries, perhaps even genital injuries, her breast described as "bruised". This was realized with greater clarity in the subsequent **Crash** novel where the author speculates on such injuries before later describing a back seat fuck resulting in "bruised vulva".[18] The film recognizes the emergence of Ballard's ideas and, although literal in its depiction of sexuality and cars, the director understands the velocity of a sex/car/trauma death eroticism.

With its soundtrack of electronic noise the film anticipates the beginning of a new music within sounds that seem to mirror the technology of cars and its annihilation in crashes; the soundtrack would find an echo a few years later in the works of the first wave industrial groups Cabaret Voltaire and Throbbing Gristle, who were similarly drawn to the late 20th century urban / suburban dystopias associated with Ballard's world, just as the first release from Mute Records, the Normal's electronic anthem "Warm Leatherette", was directly inspired by **Crash**.

The film, with its 1970s BBC production values, appears dated, the tonal palette reduced (perhaps in part to primitive video technologies and aged stock) to the beige and light brown of Ballard's suit and the car's leathery interior, the industrial grays of the urban landscape of roads, car parks, distant business parks, and the cavernous skies of west London, ensnaring the tone of Ballard's work from the era. This is the suburban world as it stretches its boundaries deeper, not just into the green belt but into the sprawling geography of the modern city; but more than that, it is stretching into the unconscious of the final years of the 20th century. Cokliss's film locates Ballard's work within this world, a world where the polymorphic perverse emerges from the return of the repressed desires of commuters as they sit behind the wheels of their cars.

NOTES

1. Emile Zola, *The Beast Within*, London: Penguin, 2007, p.66.
2. Richard von Krafft-Ebing, *Psychopathia Sexualis*, London: Velvet Publication, 1997, p.91-93.
3. J.G. Ballard, **Crash**, London: Harper Collins, 2008, p.135.
4. ibid, p.145.
5. ibid, p.148.
6. "This author is beyond psychiatric help. DO NOT PUBLISH" in Graeme Revell, 'Critique' in V. Vale & Andrea Juno, *Re/Search 8/9: J.G. Ballard*, San Francisco: Re/Search Publications, 1984. p.144.
7. **Crash**, p.166.
8. Gilles Deleuze, 'Coldness and Cruelty', in Gilles Deleuze and Leopold von Sacher-Masoch, *Masochism: Coldness And Cruelty and Venus In Furs*, New York: Zone Books, 1989, p.28.
9. J.G. Ballard, **The Atrocity Exhibition**, London: Panther Books, 1972, p.78.

10. J.G. Ballard, **The Atrocity Exhibition**, expanded and annotated edition, London: 4th Estate, 2006 (1970), p.28.
11. This show was mentioned as an idea in **The Atrocity Exhibition**, its realisation was subsequent to the writing of the disaster. Three cars were exhibited in the show: a Pontiac, a Mini and an Austin Cambridge, each of which carried their own latent meanings and symbols.
12. J.G. Ballard quoted in Jerome Tarshis, 'Krafft-Ebing Visits Dealey Plaza: The Recent Fiction Of J G Ballard' in *The Evergreen Review*, vol 17, no. 96. Spring 1973.
13. http://ftvdb.bfi.org.uk/sift/title/845040
14. Cokliss would go on to direct *It's Fantastic It's Futuristic It's Fatalistic It's Science Fiction* (1973) and *Chicago Blues* (1977) both for the BBC's *Omnibus* arts strand. He also directed feature films including as *Battletruck* (1981) and *Dream Demon* (1988).
15. J.G. Ballard quoted in V. Vale and Mike Ryan, *J.G. Ballard: Quotes*, San Francisco: Re/Search, 2004, p.242.
16. J.G. Ballard, **The Kindness Of Women**, London: Harper Perennial, 2008 (1992), p.224/5.
17. J.G. Ballard, **The Atrocity Exhibition**, p.143.
18. J.G. Ballard, **Crash**, p.135.

TRANSCRIPT OF THE FILM "CRASH!"

NARRATOR: In slow motion, the test cars moved towards each other on collision courses, unwinding behind them the coils that ran to the metering devices by the impact zone. As they collided the debris of wings and fender floated into the air. The cars rocked against each as they continued on their disintegrating courses. In the passenger seats the plastic models transcribed graceful arcs into the buckling roofs and windshields. Here and there a passing fender severed a torso. The air behind the cars was a carnival of arms and legs.

J.G. BALLARD: I think the key image of the 20th century is the man in the motor car. It sums up everything: the elements of speed, drama, aggression, the junction of advertising and consumer goods with the technological landscape. The sense of violence and desire, power and energy; the shared experience of moving together through an elaborately signalled landscape.

We spend a substantial part of our lives in the motor car, and the experience of driving condenses many of the experiences of being a human being in the 1970s, the marriage of the physical aspects of ourselves with the imaginative and technological aspects of our lives. I think the 20th century reaches its highest expression on the highway. Everything is there: the speed and violence of our age; the strange love affair with the machine, with its own death.

The styling of motor cars, and of the American motor car in particular, has always struck me as incredibly important, bringing together all sorts of visual and psychological factors. As an engineering structure, the car is totally uninteresting to me. I'm interested in the exact way in which it brings together the visual codes for expressing our ordinary perceptions about reality – for example, that the future is something with a fin on it – and the whole system of expectations contained in the design of the car, expectations about our freedom to move through time and space, about the identities of our own bodies, our own musculatures, the complex relationships between ourselves and the world of objects around us. These highly potent visual codes can be seen repeatedly in every aspect of the 20th century landscape. What do they mean? Have we reached a point now in the 70s where we only make sense in terms of these huge technological systems? I think so myself, and that it is the vital job of the writer to try to analyse and understand the huge significance of this metallised dream.

I'm interested in the automobile as a narrative structure, as a scenario that describes our real lives and our real fantasies. If every member of the human race were to vanish overnight, I think it would be possible to reconstitute almost every element of human psychology from the design of a vehicle like this. As a writer I feel I must try to understand the real meaning of a lot of commonplace but tremendously complicated events. I've always been fascinated by the complexity of movement when a woman gets out of a car.

NARRATOR: Her ungainly transit across the passenger seat through the nearside door. The overlay of her knees with the metal door flank. The conjunction of the aluminized gutter trim with the volumes of her thighs. The crushing of her left breast by the door frame, and its self extension as she continued to rise. The movement of her left hand across the chromium trim of the right headlamp assembly. Her movements distorted in the projecting carapace of the bonnet. The jut and rake of her pubis as she sits in the driver's seat. The soft pressure of her thighs against the rim of the steering wheel.

J.G. BALLARD: The close relationship between our own bodies and the body of the motor car is obvious. American automobile stylists have been exploring for years the relationship between sexuality and the motor car body, the primitive algebra of recognition which we use in our perception of all organic forms. If the man in the motor car is the key image of the 20th century, then the automobile crash is the most significant trauma. The car crash is the most dramatic event in most people's lives, apart from their own deaths, and in many cases the two will coincide.

Are we just victims in a totally meaningless tragedy, or does it in fact take place with our unconscious, and even conscious, connivance? Each year hundreds of thousands of people are killed in car crashes all over the world. Millions are injured. Are these arranged deaths arranged by the colliding forces of the technological landscape, by our own unconscious fantasies about power and aggression, our obsessions with consumer goods and desires, the overlaying fictions that are more and more taking the place of reality? It's always struck me that people's attitudes towards the car crash are very confused, that they assume an attitude that in fact is very different from their real response. If we really feared the car crash, none of us would ever be able to drive a car.

I know that my own attitudes to the crashed car are just as confused. The distorted geometry of this tremendously stylised object: let's face it, the most powerful symbol of our civilisation. It seems to pull at all sorts of concealed triggers in the mind: the postures of people in crashed vehicles; deformed manufacturer's styling devices (crashed General Motors cars look very different from crashed Fords); the stylisation of the instrument panel, which after all is the model for our own wounds. Driving around, each of us knows what is literally the shape of our own death.

NARRATOR: Regaining consciousness, she stared at the blood on her legs. The heavy liquid pulled at her skirt. The bruise under her left breast reached behind her sternum, seizing like a hand at her heart. She sat up, lifting herself from the broken steering wheel, uncertain for a moment whether the car windshield had been fractured. Against her forehead the strands of blood formed a torn veil. Above her knees, her hand moved towards the door lever. As she watched, the door opened and she fell out. Lifting herself, she held tightly to the car, feeling the pressure of the door slip against her hand. Turning, she stared at the waiting figure of the man she knew to be Dr Tallis.

J.G. BALLARD: I remember seeing some films on television of test crashes a few years ago. They were using American cars of the late 50s, a period I suppose when the American dream, and American confidence, were at their highest point. Metering coils trailed out of the windows and they had dummies sitting in them. They were beautifully filmed. They filmed them beautifully because they wanted to know what was happening. They weren't interested in the aesthetics of the thing. These cars were in head-on collisions, right-angled collisions and sideswipes. And ploughing into other structures like utility poles. One could see four feet of metal suddenly become one foot. Filmed in slow motion, these crashes had a beautiful stylised grace. The power and weight of these cars gave them an immense classical dignity. It was like some strange technological ballet.

I remember looking at these films and thinking about the strange psychological dimensions they seemed to touch. They seemed to say something about the way everything becomes more and more stylised, more and more cut off from ordinary feeling. It seems to me that we have to regard everything in the world around us as fiction, as if we were living in an enormous novel, and that the kind of distinction that Freud made about the inner world of the mind, between, say, what dreams appeared to be and what they really meant, now has to be applied to the outer world of reality. All the structures in it, flyovers and motorways, office blocks and factories, are all part of this enormous novel.

Take a structure like a multi-storey car park, one of the most mysterious buildings ever built. Is it a model for some strange psychological state, some kind of vision glimpsed within its bizarre geometry? What effect does using these buildings have on us? Are the real myths of this century being written in terms of these huge unnoticed structures?

More exactly, I think that new emotions and new feelings are being created, that modern technology is beginning to reach into our dreams and change our whole way of looking at things, and perceiving reality, that more and more it is drawing us away from contemplating ourselves to contemplating its world.

A PSYCHOPATHIC HYMN: J.G. BALLARD'S "CRASHED CARS" EXHIBITION 1970

AN ESSAY BY SIMON FORD

'For him these wounds were the keys to a new sexuality born from a perverse technology. The images of these wounds hung in the gallery of his mind like exhibits in the museum of a slaughterhouse.'[1]

In 1958 the assistant editor of *Chemistry And Industry*, a journal published by the Society of the Chemical Industry, produced a series of text-based collages. **Project For A New Novel** consisted of four double page spreads, with typeface borrowed from the American magazine *Chemical and Engineering News*. The author, J.G. Ballard, later described the work as 'sample pages of a new kind of novel, entirely consisting of magazine-style headlines and layouts, with a deliberately meaningless text, the idea being that the imaginative content could be carried by the headlines and overall design.'[2] Martin Bax, editor of the literary magazine *Ambit*, recalled that Ballard's initial plan for the collages was to have them enlarged and put on billboards: 'What he said was – what people read nowadays is advertising, so if you want to have novels that people read, you should publish them as advertisements!'[3] Over the years the collages, with their mentions of characters such as Kline, Coma and Xero, proved to be uncannily prescient of Ballard's subsequent interests.

This early indication of Ballard's fascination with the culture of publicity culminated in the late sixties with a series of self-produced advertisements for various literary magazines. Rather than advertise a particular product, such as his latest book, Ballard instead produced enigmatic juxtapositions of image and text that resembled mini-prospectuses for future novels. Likening himself to a brand he credited them as 'A J.G. Ballard Production'. The 1967 advertisement **Does The Angle Between Two Walls Have A Happy Ending?** was typical, with its combination of a film still (a low-angle high-contrast photograph of a woman with her hand covering her genitals) and the text: 'Fiction is a branch of neurology: the scenarios of nerve and blood vessel are the written mythologies of memory and desire. Sex: Inner Space: J.G. Ballard.'[4] The text conformed to Ballard's oft-stated assertion that the imagination of the science fiction writer was best directed away from fantasies of exploring outer space in favour of an exploration of the internal landscape of the mind.[5]

Ballard produced all the artwork for the advertisements himself and in all dealings with the magazines acted exactly like a commercial client. He initially wanted to place them in upmarket magazines such as *Vogue* or *Paris Match*, but soon realised he could only afford to publish them in smaller literary magazine such as *Ambit* and *New Worlds*.[6] To subsidise his costs Ballard applied to the Arts Council for a £1,000 grant. According to the *Sunday Times* the advertisements would have featured 'a nude on Westminster Abbey's high altar, a motor crash, and Princess Margaret's left armpit.'[7] The Arts Council eventually refused the application, perhaps mindful of Ballard's increasingly controversial subject matter epitomised by the title of his latest text for *Ambit*: **Plan For The Assassination Of Jacqueline Kennedy**.[8]

Ballard's interest in advertising imagery complimented his enthusiasm for Pop Art, especially works by Andy Warhol and the Scottish artist, Eduardo Paolozzi. Ballard first met Paolozzi in 1966 when, along with Michael Moorcock, he visited the artist to discuss his possible involvement in the science fiction magazine *New Worlds*. Ballard and Paolozzi subsequently became friends, not least because they shared a fascination with the imagery and artefacts of consumer society and its mass-produced popular culture. Works such as Paolozzi's 1964 sculpture "Crash" (an assemblage of various pipes and cylinders) could be seen as analogous to the fragmentary texts that Ballard was then starting to produce and that he would eventually collect together in 1970 for **The Atrocity Exhibition**.[9]

In May 1968 Ballard was planning, along with Paolozzi and the psychologist Dr Christopher Evans, to produce a play at the Institute of Contemporary Arts (ICA) entitled *Crash*, featuring a crashed car. As described at the time by June Rose in the *Sunday Mirror*: 'all the horror and realism of an actual road smash will be played out in front of the audience. The young driver, in blood-covered track suit, will lie beside the mangled car. His girl friend will kneel beside him, caressing him. Dummies will mouth words about the beautiful and desirable features of the motor car. Behind them, film of cars crashing will make up the stark and terrible accompaniment.'[10] According to Rose's description the production would feature crash-test dummies by Paolozzi and a meta-commentary narrated by Evans. The narrative developed by Ballard involved a young man buying his first car, his death in a car crash and his subsequent transformation into a victim-hero. For Ballard the play demonstrated how car crashes had the effect of 'liberating sexual libido, radiating the sexuality and energy of the victim who died in an intensity impossible in any other form.'[11]

Crash, the play, never came to fruition but another adaptation of Ballard's work did take place at the ICA just over a year later in August 1969. Without his direct involvement a group of architects, designers and Lambda actors put on a mixed media production of his 1966 short story, **The Assassination Weapon**. *Punch*'s Jeremy Kingston described the ambitious and complicated production: 'In the centre of the room a large white disc slowly rotates. Projectors in the four corners flash images on to this double screen while a voice sonorously reads passages by the ex-science-fiction writer J.G. Ballard... The superimposed photographs, surrealist paintings, charts and mandalas coupled with Ballard's dense distressed sentences have the texture of an unhappy dream. A Max Ernst worldscape of mighty fragments – flyovers, deserts, dark reservoirs, radio-telescopes – following the private logic of an hallucinating mind. Puzzling, frequently powerful, devised and invented with ingenuity and skill.'[12]

The many projects, collaborations and adaptations outlined above serve to indicate that although Ballard's main focus was his short story and novel writing he also harbored ambitions to operate in the wider cultural field. In particular, despite *Crash* the play being abandoned, he continued to develop his ideas about the cultural meaning of car crashes. The next form this research took was as an exhibition at the recently opened New Arts Lab at 1 Robert Street in London. Adjacent to the busy Hampstead Road and opposite an imposing high-rise housing estate, it was situated in just the kind of post-industrial hinterland that Ballard frequently featured in his fiction.[13] He described the space as 'a one-time pharmaceutical warehouse; its open concrete decks were the perfect setting for its brutalist happenings and exhibitions, its huge ventilation shafts purpose-built to evacuate the last breath of pot smoke in the event of a drugs raid.'[14]

The New Arts Lab had been set up by a group of dissidents recently associated with the first Arts Lab in Covent Garden.[15] With Camden Council they negotiated a short-lease arrangement for the building and set up IRAT (Institute for Research in Art & Technology) to manage the space. Amongst the trustees were Ballard, Reyner Banham, Dr Christopher Evans, Richard W. Evans, Cllr. Christine Stewart and artist Joe Tilson. The Rt. Hon. Lord Harlech acted as Patron and Lord Burgh as Sponsor. The Directors in August 1970 were listed as Lance Blackstone, David Curtis, Hugh Davies, Fred Drummond, John Hopkins, Rosemary Johnson, David Kilburn, Malcolm Le Grice, Diane Lifton, John Lifton, Carla Liss (USA), Joebear Webb, Pamela Zoline (USA) with Biddy Peppin as Secretary.[16]

IRAT encouraged cross-disciplinary work in cinema, video, print, theatre, music, photography and cybernetics. The gallery space was officially opened on 4 October 1969 and featured a poetry writing machine attached to a nearby teleprinter and another computer in Great Portland Street.[17] The gallery shared the ground floor of the building with a small cinema and in the weeks leading up to Ballard's exhibition the New Arts Lab's programme included screenings of Andy Warhol's films and an exhibition by Ian Breakwell and John Hilliard.[18]

As advertised in *Art & Artists*, 'Jim Ballard: Crashed Cars' took place at the gallery between 4-28 April 1970.[19] The cars – a Pontiac, an Austin Cambridge A60 and a Mini – were hired from Charles Symmonds's knacker's yard, Motor Crash Repairs. 'They don't appeal to me as art,' Symmonds told the Sunday Times. 'I detest cars. But maybe it's a good idea to show crashed cars. It's frightening.'[20] Ballard's choice of car was far from accidental. The Pontiac was a model from the mid-fifties, and thus represented a particularly baroque phase in American car styling, while the Mini symbolised the fun-loving mobility of the swinging sixties. The sober and conservative saloon, the A60, stood for the Mini's exact antithesis.[21] All however, through the catastrophe of the car crash, were now in a sense equivalent; smashed and levelled to the raw material of their crushed metal, broken glass, and stained upholstery.[22]

Ballard's decision to focus on such a traumatic event and the presentation of its aftermath as an artwork proved particularly challenging to its audience. For Ballard cars were the key symbol of the 20th century. In 1971 he described them as encapsulating 'speed, drama and aggression, the worlds of advertising and consumer goods, engineering and mass manufacture, and the shared experience of moving together through an elaborately signalled landscape.'[23] Ballard was not, of course, the first artist to celebrate and recognise the significance of the motorcar. Precedents exist from the early days of avant-gardism. Take, for example, Filippo Tommaso Marinetti's 'The Foundation and Manifesto of Futurism' (1909) with its celebration of the 'beauty of speed' and its assertion that 'a roaring car that seems to ride on grapeshot is more beautiful than the Victory of Samothrace.'[24] Cars also featured as subject matter and raw material in the post-war sculpture of the American artist John Chamberlain and the Nouveaux Réaliste artist César Baldaccini. Examples of works specifically relating to car crashes include Jim Dine's happening, "The Car Crash", held at the Reuben Gallery, New York, in 1960 and Andy Warhol's car crash screenprints of 1963. Also in 1963 Arman created White Orchid, a fully functional white MG convertible sports car, dynamited in a quarry near Düsseldorf and then exhibited pinned to a wall. It is uncertain whether Ballard knew of these precedents, although he was certainly aware of the American artist Ed Keinholz and his work 'Back Seat Dodge 38' because he described it with some relish in **The Atrocity Exhibition** as 'a wrecked white car with the plastic dummies of a World War III pilot and a girl with facial burns making love among a refuse of bubblegum war cards and oral contraceptive wallets.'[25]

To make explicit some of the ideas behind 'Crashed Cars' Ballard produced an exhibition handout.

Each of these sculptures is a memorial to a unique collision between man and his technology. However tragic they are, automobile crashes play very different roles from the ones we assign them. Behind our horror lie an undeniable fascination and excitement, most clearly revealed by the deaths of the famous: Jayne Mansfield and James Dean, Albert Camus and John F. Kennedy. The 20th century has given birth to a vast range of machines – computers, pilotless planes, thermonuclear weapons – where the latent identity of the machine is ambiguous. An understanding of this identity can be found in a study of the automobile, which dominates the vectors of speed, aggression, violence and desire.

In particular, the automobile crash contains a crucial image of the machine as conceptualised psychopathology. Apart from its function of redefining the elements of space and time in terms of our most potent consumer durable, the car crash may be perceived unconsciously as a fertilising rather than a destructive event – a liberation of sexual energy – meditating the asexuality [sic] of those who have died with an intensity impossible in any other form. In 20th century terms the crucifixion would be enacted as a conceptual car crash.

The car crash is the most dramatic event we are likely to experience in our entire lives apart from our own deaths.[26]

In his fictionalised autobiography, **The Kindness Of Women**, Ballard replaced this text with one adapted from his 1974 introduction to the French edition of **Crash**. This fictionalised handout extended Ballard's analysis further, describing the sixties as the decade of the marriage of reason and nightmare, a decade dominated by 'sinister technologies.' In this new world nuclear weapons and soft-drink advertisements coexisted 'in an uneasy realm ruled by advertising and pseudo-events, science and pornography. The death of feeling and emotion has at last left us free to pursue our own psychopathologies as a game.' The exhibition, he claimed, pointed to a 'pandemic cataclysm that kills hundreds of thousands of people each year and injures millions, but is a source of endless entertainment on our film and television screens.'[27]

That he had hit upon a theme of some power became immediately apparent on the night of 3rd April when the exhibition opened. In his account of the opening party the 100-odd guests quickly became drunk, while at Ballard's invitation a topless woman circulated, interviewing members of the audience for a closed-circuit television broadcast. The incongruity of the crashed cars and this celebratory social event was further compounded by the alcohol-induced removal of social constraints and the distancing effect of guests watching themselves on closed-circuit television monitors. The result, according to Ballard, was 'nervous hysteria.'[28] Guests poured wine over the cars, broke their glasses and the topless interviewer, Ballard claimed, 'was nearly raped in the back seat of the Pontiac by some self-aggrandizing character.'[29] The exhibition continued to act as a stimulus to transgressive acts well after the opening party. In the following days visitors repeatedly attacked the cars, daubed them in paint, broke windows, tore off wing mirrors, and urinated on the seats. Such was the violence directed at the cars that the staff at Motor Crash Repairs were shocked when Ballard returned them to the yard.[30]

Although Ballard's fiction contained many examples of the conditioning effect of an environment on the psychological state of his characters, he later expressed some shock at the aggression shown towards the cars.[31] What he underestimated was the force of the reaction and the desire on the part of some visitors to continue with the process of destruction and desecration of the cars. But what the exhibition and the audience's reaction did confirm was Ballard's thesis that social relations between individuals were now increasingly complicated by our relationship with what he termed the 'technological landscape'.[32] The exhibition of crashed cars provided the opportunity to make this relationship manifest in a psychologically heightened manner. The exhibition engaged its audience in a phenomenological sense that no novel could ever hope to achieve, including Ballard's latest publication **The Atrocity Exhibition**.

Described by Roger Lockhurst as a 'bizarre exhibition catalogue'[33] **The Atrocity Exhibition** collected together works written between 1966 and 1969 for journals including *Ambit, Encounter, ICA Eventsheet* and *International Times*. In terms of experimental fiction it was Ballard's most ambitious book to date. With its non-linear narrative structure, its clinically repetitive style and its clipped short paragraphs, the book reflected Ballard's uniquely eclectic taste in what he called the 'invisible literature' of market research reports, company in-house magazines, promotional copy, press releases, science abstracts, internal memoranda, sex manuals, and government reports.[34] Ballard's original concept for **The Atrocity Exhibition** was to make it radical in both form and content. Perhaps with Paolozzi's print portfolios in mind, he had intended the book to be published in a large format and illustrated with his own collages of medical textbook and car crash imagery. The publisher Jonathan Cape, however, rejected this proposal. Ballard later complained that to them an illustrated book meant a text accompanied by a few line drawings by a distinguished artist such as Felix Topolski.[35] Ballard's publisher, however, did nothing to discourage his obsession with apparently irrational acts of violence in modern society and the complicity of the entertainment industry to turn these events into 'atrocity exhibitions'. The 'Crashed Cars' exhibition enabled Ballard to transplant this fictional world of the imagination from the page and place it in the context of a real exhibition of atrocities. This was fact following fiction. In **The Atrocity Exhibition** the main character – variously named Travers, Talbert, Travis etc – organized an exhibition of crashed cars and founded *Crash* magazine, which reproduced photographs of the mutilated bodies of celebrity car crash victims including Jayne Mansfield, Albert Camus and James Dean, creating tableaux of what Ballard described as 'epiphanies of violence and desire.'[36] Later in the book Ballard's 'Dr Nathan' attempted to explain the main character's troubled relationship with violence, and linked it specifically to 'the death of affect': 'The only way we can make contact with each other is in terms of conceptualisations. Violence is the conceptualisation of pain. By the same token psychopathology is the conceptual system of sex.'[37] The automobile crash formed the 'crucial image of the machine as conceptualised psychopathology.'[38] It soon became clear, however, that Dr Nathan's discourse formed its own type of psychopathology, a psychopathology of pornography. As an analytical process that often sought to separate matter and action from its context, the discourse of the detached scientific observer represented 'the ultimate pornography.'[39] The crashed car therefore becomes a site where the discourses of sexuality and psychopathology fuse, where we all slow down to observe 'the new logic of violence and sensation that ruled our lives.'[40] The exhibition extenuated this logic of violence because as Ballard realised, in the society of the spectacle the 'atrocity exhibition was more stirring than the atrocity.'[41]

The exhibition therefore encapsulated Ballard's key concerns at this time; in particular the death of affect resulting from our increasing alienation from direct experience. The car crash represented this by default through being one of the few dramatic acts of violence a person might witness or experience as real rather than as an imaginative act.[42] The exhibition of the 'found' and 'ready-made' crashed cars, selected but unaltered by Ballard, aimed to reproduce the associated glamour of the car crash fed to us in films and news reports. Ballard likened the exhibition to a 'psychological test', a way to examine an 'hypotheses about our unconscious fascination with car crashes and their latent sexuality.'[43] The intense reaction convinced him that the subject carried more than a limited or specialised interest and spurred him on to write his most celebrated novel, **Crash**.[44]

Situated historically as the 'sixties' became the 'seventies', the exhibition took place at a time of transition from a period characterised by optimism and increasing prosperity to one characterised by uncertainty, economic recession and crisis. In this sense Ballard's 'Crashed Cars' exhibition, like his fiction, looked forward to a future where the promised liberatory role of new technologies was overshadowed by the often deadly consequences of that same technological 'progress'. Cars would continue to be death traps, the logic of their moving parts dedicated to their own, and periodically our, obsolescence. Like the novel it inspired the 'Crashed Cars' exhibition revealed cars as objects of both consecration and desecration, instant relics of a new but powerful anti-humanist force in society.

In his introduction to the novel **Crash** Ballard described his aspiration to write as if he were a scientist faced with the unknown: 'All he can do is to devise various hypotheses and test them against the facts.'[45] But despite this disinterested stance Ballard also claimed for **Crash** a moral message: 'the ultimate role of *Crash* is cautionary, a warning against the brutal, erotic and overlit realm that beckons more and more persuasively to us from the margins of the technological landscape.'[46] For Jean Baudrillard this did not make for a convincing argument. For Baudrillard the true 'miracle' of **Crash** lay in its rejection of the 'moral gaze': 'Crash is hypercritical, in the sense of being beyond the critical.'[47] Ballard later modified his position on **Crash** and came to recognise that perhaps it was not a cautionary tale after all: '*Crash* is what it appears to be. It is a psychopathic hymn.'[48]

NOTES

1. J.G. Ballard, **Crash**, London: Vintage, 1995, p.13. First published 1973.
2. Vale and Andrea Juno (eds.), *J. G. Ballard*, San Francisco: Re/Search, 1984, p.38.
3. 'Interview with Martin Bax' in: Vale and Juno (eds.), 1984, op cit., p.39. It took another twenty years before this work was published in a magazine. See J.G. Ballard, 'Zero Synthesis...', *New Worlds*, no. 213, Summer 1978.
4. *Ambit*, no. 33, 1967. The advertisement was also published in *New Worlds*, no. 178, December 1967. The film still came from *Alone* by Steve Dwoskin. Ballard's appreciation of Dwoskin's films led to his providing the text for 'The Bathroom: A Film In Progress by Steve Dwoskin', in *The Running Man*, vol. 1, no. 2, July-Aug 1968. The other advertisements were: **Homage To Claire Churchill**, Ambit, no. 32, 1967 (also published on the inside front cover of New Worlds, no. 176, October 1967); **A Neural Interval**, *Ambit*, no. 36, 1968 (also published in *New Worlds*, no. 185, December 1968); **Placental Insufficiency**, *Ambit*, no. 45, 1970; and **Venus Smiles**, *Ambit*, no. 46, 1970/1971.
5. This position can be usefully compared to Alexander Trocchi's contemporary project to become a 'cosmonaut of inner space', see Andrew Murray Scott (ed.), *Alexander Trocchi: Invisible Insurrection of a Million Minds: A Trocchi Reader*, Edinburgh: Polygon, 1991.
6. Ballard in: Vale and Juno (eds.), p.147.
7. Anon. 'J.G. Ballard: Advertising Is the Medium', *Sunday Times*, 19 October 1967. Extract quoted in: David Pringle, *J.G. Ballard: A Primary & Secondary Bibliography*, Boston, Mass.: G.K. Hall & Co., 1984, p.89.
8. *Ambit*, no. 31, 1967. Ballard appears to have half-expected the Arts Council's refusal

of the application: 'Sadly, I ran out of cash, and my half-serious application for a grant... was turned down'. J.G. Ballard, **The Atrocity Exhibition**, San Francisco: Re/Search Publications, 1990, pp.46-47.

9. J.G. Ballard, **The Atrocity Exhibition**, London: Jonathan Cape, 1970. By 1970 Ballard and Paolozzi were closely involved in each other's practice. For example Ballard wrote the introductory text for Paolozzi's *General Dynamic Fun* portfolio of 1970 and Ballard also knew of Paolozzi's collection of crash test dummy photographs. Paolozzi made use of this material in five etchings entitled 'Mannikins for Destruction' in the portfolio *Conditional Probability Machine* (1970), printed by Alecto Studios, London. He also used a dummy's head in the sculpture 'Crash Head' (1971), now in the Krazy Kat Arkive, Victoria & Albert Museum. See: Robin Spencer (ed.) *Eduardo Paolozzi: Writings and Interviews*, Oxford: Oxford University Press, 2000, p.204. Another experimental work by Ballard that drew on the visual arts from this period included his concrete poem, **Love: A Print-out For Claire Churchill** (1968), first published in *Ambit*, no. 37, 1968, p.9.

10. June Rose, 'If Christ Came Again He Would Be Killed In A Car Crash', *Sunday Mirror*, 19 May 1968.

11. Ibid.

12. Jeremy Kingston, 'At The Theatre', *Punch*, 20 August 1969, pp.313-314. Transcribed in Pringle, p.91. The short story was first published as: **The Assassination Weapon**, *New Worlds*, 49, no. 161, April 1966, pp.4-12. Revised edition published in: J.G. Ballard, **The Atrocity Exhibition**, St Albans: Panther, 1972, pp.37-46. First published 1970.

13. See Ballard's **Concrete Island**, London: Jonathan Cape, 1974 and **High Rise**, London: Jonathan Cape, 1975. Rather fittingly, considering Ballard's interest in ruins and memories, the building has since been demolished and the site buried beneath an extension of the high-rise housing estate.

14. This description comes from his fictional autobiography, **The Kindness Of Women**, London: Flamingo, 1994, p.223. There may be some poetic licence at work here as, according to David Curtis and Biddy Peppin, there were no ventilation shafts at Gordon Street (information from David Curtis, conversation with author, 19 January 2005).

15. Opened in July 1967 by Jim Haynes, the Arts Lab on Drury Lane housed not only an exhibition space but also a cinema and refectory. Such amenities made it perfect for live events and 'happenings' and helped establish it as the quintessential drop-in/drop-out centre of the London counter-culture. Despite its closure in the winter of 1969, it provided a model for many new art centres that opened throughout Britain in the early 1970s, including the New Arts Lab.

16. From headed paper in the IRAT papers in the British Artists' Film & Video Study Collection in Central St. Martins. For an account of the Lab's guiding principles see: John Hopkins, 'New Arts Lab', *Friends*, no. 5, 14 April 1970, p.9.

17. See John Hopkins, 'Telecompint' [sic], *Friends*, no. 4, March 1970, p.12. This event was also covered in the *Hampstead and Highgate Express*, 10 October 1969, where Ballard was mentioned as a guest. The archives of IRAT can be found in the British Artists' Film & Video Study Collection at Central St Martins College of Art and Design. The Gordon Street space finally closed on 26 March 1971 when Camden Council reclaimed the building. IRAT Ltd. continued and set up a new space at 15 Prince of Wales Crescent, London, NW1 8HA, where it operated till at least April 1972.

18. The Breakwell and Hilliard exhibition opened on 28 February and closed on 21 March 1970. Prior to this exhibition the gallery had been closed for extensive renovation work. At this time the shows were arranged by Pamela Zoline, Biddy Peppin, Liz Ewens and Godfrey Rubens. After Ballard's exhibition came 'Diagrams/Similes: Judith Clark' and 'Things in the World: Pamela Zoline', 5-25 June 1970, and then an exhibition by the Italian art group Amodulo, 'Amodulo Art', 31 June – 19 July 1970.
19. *Art & Artists*, April 1970, p.40.
20. Quoted from: Pringle, op cit., p.92. In **The Kindness Of Women** the cars became a Peugeot, a Mini and a black Lincoln Continental, identical to President Kennedy's limousine. See: Ballard, 1994, p.226.
21. A white Pontiac also featured in Ballard's **The Atrocity Exhibition**. In a note added to this book he explained why he was particularly interested in this car: 'Why a white Pontiac? A British pop star of the 1960s, Dicky Valentine, drove his daughter in a white Pontiac to the same school that my own children attended near the film studios at Shepperton. The car had a powerful iconic presence, emerging from all those American movies into the tranquil TV suburbs. Soon after, Valentine died in a car accident.' Ballard, 1990, op cit., p.9.
22. A photograph (credited to Hulton Getty) of the smashed up Pontiac with a women sitting in the passenger seat holding up a hand-painted sign '£3000' can be seen in: Rugoff, Ralph. 'Dangerous Driving: J.G. Ballard interviewed by Ralph Rugoff', *Frieze*, no. 34, 1997, pp.48-53.
23. 'The Car, The Future', in: J.G. Ballard, *Users' Guide to the Millennium*, London: Flamingo, 1996, p.262. First published in *Drive*, 1971.
24. Filippo Tommaso Marinetti's 'The Foundation and Manifesto of Futurism' (1909) in Charles Harrison and Paul Wood (eds.), *Art in Theory: 1900-2000: An Anthology of Ideas*, Oxford: Blackwell Publishing, 2003, p.147.
25. Ballard, 1972, p.16. First published 1970.
26. Transcribed in: Jo Stanley, 'Ballard Crashes', *Friends*, no. 7, 29 May 1970, pp.4-5. This handout text is based on passages that also appeared in Ballard's **The Atrocity Exhibition**, see Ballard, 1972, p.125. The phrase quoted above, 'meditating the asexuality...', appears in **The Atrocity Exhibition** as 'mediating the sexuality...'.
27. Ballard, 1994, p.226.
28. Ballard, 1990, p.25. This was not the last time Ballard worked with scantily clad women. For a few years after the exhibition the professional stripper, Euphoria Bliss, could be found at events reading, naked, extracts from his work. A photograph of Euphoria performing watched by the male members of the *Ambit* staff, including Ballard, was published on the front cover of the magazine (no. 50) in 1972.
29. Ballard quoted in: Eduardo Paolozzi, J.G. Ballard and Frank Whitford, 'Speculative Illustrations', Studio International, 1971, vol. 182, pp.136–143. Ballard's memory of the exhibition may have informed an episode that takes place in his later novel **Cocaine Nights** where a group of onlookers assemble to witness a violent assault: 'They had watched the rape attempt without intervening, like a gallery audience at an exclusive private view.' J.G. Ballard, **Cocaine Nights**, London: Flamingo, 1997, p.58.
30. Ballard, 1994, p.230.
31. Paolozzi, Ballard, and Whitford, 1971.
32. J.G. Ballard, 'Fictions of Every Kind', in Vale and Juno (eds.), 1984, p.99. Article first

published, *Books and Bookmen*, February 1971.
33. Roger Lockhurst, *The Angle Between Two Walls: The Fiction of J.G. Ballard*, Liverpool: Liverpool University Press, 1997, p.74.
34. J.G. Ballard, 'Quotations by Ballard', in Vale and Juno (eds.), 1984, p.156. This list comes from an article first published in *Books and Bookmen*, 9 July 1970.
35. Ballard quoted in David Pringle 'From Shanghai to Shepperton', in Vale and Juno (eds.), 1984, p.124. Interview first published in *Foundation*, no. 24, February 1982.
36. Ballard, 1972, p.30.
37. Ibid., pp.93-94.
38. Ibid., p.124.
39. Ibid., p.44.
40. Ballard, 1994, p.226.
41. Ibid., p.119.
42. Ballard was himself involved in a car crash, not long after the publication of **Crash**, when his Ford Zephyr blew a tyre on the motorway, hit the central barrier, rolled over and was narrowly missed by oncoming traffic.
43. Quoted in: Hans Ulrich Obrist, *Interviews: Volume 1*. Milan: Charta, 2003, pp.61-62.
44. See a note on the exhibition in: Ballard, 1990, p.25.
45. Ballard, 1995, p.6.
46. Ibid., p.6.
47. Jean Baudrillard, 'Ballard's Crash,' *Science Fiction Studies*, no. 55, vol. 18, part 3, November 1991, pp.309-19. See also Nicholas Ruddick's response 'Ballard/Crash/Baudrillard', *Science Fiction Studies*, no. 58, vol. 19, part 3, November 1992, pp.354-60.
48. Ballard in: Will Self, *Junk Mail*, London: Penguin, 1996, p.369.

CONFLICTED IMAGES: BALLARD AND PAOLOZZI AT WAR

AN ESSAY BY CHRIS HORROCKS

The highest praise I could give to Paolozzi is to say that if the entire 20th century were to vanish in some huge calamity, it would be possible to reconstitute a large part of it from his sculpture and screenprints.[1]

In Runnymede, Surrey, an acre of land is the territory of the United States of America. At the peak of the landscaped knoll lies the 1965 JFK memorial sculpture.[2] In 1968 this huge, engraved block suffered bomb damage, a protest against the Vietnam War or, a newspaper report surmised, Jackie Kennedy's plans for re-marriage.[3]

The monument inspired J.G. Ballard's 1969 short story **The Killing Ground**. Its protagonist, Pearson, a major in the British National Liberation Army, fights an occupying force from the United States. Captured US soldiers, including an architect from the US Army Graves Commission, have been sent to retrieve the seven-ton stone. Before their execution the architect cleans the monument, exposing years of anti-US graffiti and vandalism. Now gleamingly exposed, the edifice becomes the signal for a hiding American platoon to wipe out the remaining rebels as they move towards the river.[4]

Ballard placed the artist Eduardo Paolozzi's art within this context of the recovered artefact: sculpture as disinterred remains revealing the fractures and fault-lines cutting through the landscape of late-twentieth-century culture. Between the actual bomb damage of the JFK memorial, its appearance in that early story, and Paolozzi's increasingly alienated relationship to the American culture he embraced as a child, the end of the 1960s saw the two artists begin to conduct a relatively short-lived critical engagement with the United States as political subject matter, quite contradicting their earlier relationship to that country. It affected their work and its reception. By 1967 Eduardo Paolozzi's disillusion with the American culture he had embraced in his earlier career as proto-pop artist was reaching its height: 'The political climate of Vietnam overshadows print series such as

Universal Electronic Vacuum of 1967 in which elegant computer language is used ironically to represent fighter-plane insignia and bombs as the agencies of war.'[5] One print, 'War Games Revisited' depicts arrays of bombs and warplanes like some insane circuit diagram or model kit plan. While the spectre of the war cut across the work of Paolozzi and Ballard, it appeared not as a sustained or coherent representation within the art and literature, but a round of skirmishes characterised by their collaged engagements using material extracted from behind enemy lines. This 'invisible literature', which Ballard said he and Paolozzi were compiling as a 'research library' in the 1970s, comprised 'bizarre verbal collages taken from fashion magazines, weapons, technology, stock market reports and so on'.[6] The elements of American culture used in these images were sinister harbingers of the contemporary alliance between culture, technology and war; a world away from the US bubble-gum cards and poster pin-ups of their childhoods.

INTERNS

As children each artist turned collecting into a meaningful project, prior to and during WWII. For Ballard, this involved his role as gofer in a Japanese internment camp outside Shanghai: '100 errands to run in return for an old copy of the photo magazine *Life* or an unwanted screwdriver'.[7] In this world the slightest thing took on great value. In Leith, Edinburgh, the young Paolozzi, from Italian parentage, collected cigarette cards and Meccano magazines. As a child he had used scrapbooks to collide visual and textual matter: for him the cheap paper was the scene where the levelling capacity of mass reproduction soldered high art imagery, product advertising, banner headlines, popular mechanics, sci-fi posters and pin-up titillation. However, once Italy had declared war, Paolozzi's family were interned as enemy aliens, and the young Eduardo was confined in a local police station. His father was lost in the terrible sinking of the ship

Paolozzi and Ballard had been friends since the mid-1960s. Known for their work in art and literature, they had a great interest in each other's discipline, in the use of techniques in film, graphics and installation art, combining images, texts and objects, as mixed media. Ballard, while experimenting with art, and being particularly interested in Surrealist painting, chose to chart a path in his writing from a technologically oriented science fiction (with roots in Surrealist imagery) to a 'science-fiction of the present', where the persistent attention to the current social order and its mores would reveal a stranger world than all his earlier literary visions of flooded cityscapes, desert resorts and crystallised jungles. Paolozzi, nominally printer and sculptor, worked in media that permitted him to forage more widely, producing books of images and found texts, and prints combining typography and photography, in a lexicon more diverse than Ballard's adherence to the printed word. Paolozzi's art, with its use of retrieved images and strange juxtapositions, posited an everyday world that required no imposed fantasy. Both artists concurred that the world often provided sufficient capacity for extremes without the addition of artistic interpretation. The duty of each was to recruit and recompile elements that were already present, in order to send them to their limits.

Their symbolic reaction to the world, conceived as a stockpile of existing material to which nothing imaginary need be applied, met with another more insistent demand, one not easily assimilated in the dynamics of fiction, fantasy and reality: the Vietnam War. For a few years, their engagement with images and narratives of war condensed around the USA's intervention in South East Asia, and the conflict seemed to disrupt their work, insofar as they attempted to introduce it as a theme with varying degrees of success. The conflict threw the artists into an area that would both lead to a departure from their earlier investments in pop and sci-fi and meet with bafflement and criticism in the 1970s. Paolozzi's exhibition, a retrospective at Tate Gallery in 1971, and Ballard's writings that led to his novel, **Crash**, were misunderstood or rejected. Their approach to the relationship between literature, art and world, once the actual violence of the USA's military and political nightmares from Vietnam to Watergate became clear, meant that the relatively restrained content of the artists' work in the 1950s and early 1960s, gave way to more politically strident output that arguably failed to find sufficient resonance or impact in their chosen media.

VIOLENT MEDIA

There is a photograph taken in 1971 of Ballard and Paolozzi in a World War 2 Jeep in the Imperial War Museum, London. Another depicts them admiring a spacesuit in the Science Museum. Paolozzi never learnt to drive, but loved cars and machinery. Ballard sits in the driver's seat, and in that year had appeared in a film based on his writings on cars, sex and death that would result in **Crash**, in 1973. The themes of war and the violence of technology permeated the work of

Ballard and Paolozzi in the late 1960s and early 1970s, and combined with their mutual interest in multi-media, montage and other ways of demolishing the boundaries between images, texts, fictions and realities, driving the artists beyond the genres with which they had previously been associated: Ballard and science fiction, Paolozzi and pop art. Indeed, it could be argued that the termination of the 1960s saw a radical if unrecognised shift in the two men's relationship not just with their chosen media, but with the themes they embraced. Such a transition brought into collision the residing preoccupations of the two artists with the articulation of fiction and reality within their chosen disciplines.

They had first encountered each other in 1966 through the sci-fi publication *New Worlds*, in which Ballard had researched a radical collage **Project For A New Novel** (1957). Ballard had also been interested in the work of the Independent Group, with which Paolozzi had been involved. The writer also made similar work for *Ambit* magazine, which involved contributors such as Jeff Nuttall and Edwin Brock. *Ambit* fused radical literature and montage, splicing the roles of writer and artist, and was the test bed for radical fiction, such as the pieces later collected in Ballard's **The Atrocity Exhibition**. Ballard began to work with *Ambit*'s editor Dr. Martin Bax on Paolozzi's major graphic series *Moonstrips Empire News/General Dynamic F.U.N* (*Ambit* #33, 1967). Paolozzi, an obsessive collector of images taken from magazines, books and newspapers, reconstructed them in montage, in what McLuhan called the 'verbi-voco-visual' complexity that defined the fractured, multi-spatial and non-linear world of contemporary culture and technology. Jennifer Baxter observed that 'art would, with its semiotics of chaos, be confrontational and produce a variety of responses. The melding and clashing of symbol and icon was paralleled by the merger of media forms, and the "multi-media" event.'[8]

Since the early 1960s Paolozzi and Ballard were absorbed by the other's medium, or rather with their mergence within the orbit of multi-media. Paolozzi created collage using text as well as image. His art book *Kex*, edited by Richard Hamilton and taking its title from the name of a Swedish candy bar, exploited extracts from works on rocketry, philosophy and biology to disturb conventional sense and promote associative meanings. He also produced an art book called *Abba Zaba* in an edition of 500 in 1970. The book comprised disparate photographs, including ones of the Pope, a super-intelligent pig, and tape recording machines, accompanied by Paolozzi's short poems. As the painter

David Pelham testified, this unique publication evidenced 'the Ballardian highways, the high-rise concrete blocks, the wrecked automobiles, corpse-strewn beaches and scenes of violent unrest, military intervention and shattered landscapes alarmingly juxtaposed with incongruous photographs of smiling pin-ups and domestic scenes'.[9] For example, in a poem echoing earlier Ballardian prose, Paolozzi writes of New York, juxtaposed with a photography of monolithic tape recording equipment: 'Out of crepuscular space its twinkling skyline ebbs, flows in tides of rainbows, greens and torrid blues, a riot of phantasmagoria'. Conversely, as early as 1964 Paolozzi had produced an aluminium sculpture called *Crash*, predating Ballard's infamous literary work. Each artist was closely aware of the other's working methods and interests.

The synthesis of media, matter and technology in Ballard's projects in the visual and performing arts began with plans to stage the car-crash components of his novel **The Atrocity Exhibition** in late 1968. It was replaced instead with a *son et lumière* exhibition of rotating disks, voice-overs and post-Surrealist themes of death, technology and desire. The culmination of this Gordian knot of techno-pathology was the staging of the show that tested the limits of audience violence and sexual excess prior to writing the novel **Crash**: 'an exhibition of crashed cars at the New Arts Laboratory in London – three crashed cars in a formal gallery ambience.'[10] Paolozzi was asked to be involved but had no time to take part. He would have contributed sculpture rather than the prints and collages and writings that had most closely associated him with the early British pop art movement. The artist had planned to provide work based on test crash dummies, as his current work included etchings on amongst other subjects *Manikins For Destruction* (1970), which used sources from original images of traffic accident simulations. This collision of the human, the machine and the trauma had been present in his work on the human form since his *Mr Cruikshank* series of busts of 1950 onwards, which took inspiration from *National Geographic* photographs of model heads used to illustrate the effects of radiation on tumours at Massachusetts Institute of Technology, and damaged test dummies from atomic bomb detonations in the Nevada desert.[11]

Paolozzi used sculpture to produce busts and statues that invoked the torn but recompiled figure of the human in the wake of the technology of war, and the violence of technology; Ballard transcended science-fiction to dissect the actual horror of our own constructed fictions, awful projections of an uninhabitable world in which we choose to exist as if living our lives as pathologies. In each case, fracture, de- and re-composition and the attempt by the artist to bring into proximity uncertain realities to provoke their fictions were central. However, the relationship of the real and fiction, posed mainly in terms of Surrealism and pop, was different in each case. Paolozzi was more comfortable with being labelled a Surrealist, owing to his exposure to the form in late 1940s Paris, and his subsequent desire to distance himself from his association with nascent British pop art and what arguably seemed the American dream he had glimpsed as a child in Edinburgh, which had rapidly become the nightmare of American domestic and foreign policy. Paolozzi had visited the US, but his time there led to a disengagement with all things American. Ballard identified a parallel transformation in this later work of Paolozzi: 'From his early sculpture, where he was using the technique appropriate at the time of overlaying an external reality, the world of nuts and bolts technology, with his own fantasies, he's gone round now to the opposite position. He is now analyzing external fictions.'[12] According to Ballard, whereas once the Surrealist technique of imposing interior fantasies onto external reality dominated, now the external reality maintained its own fictive dimension, which impinged on the structures of the mind. This reversal, which Ballard saw as central to his own writing, led to an analytic rather than synthetic encounter with the world. Rather than combining elements of the real in order to impose an interpretation stemming from the desire of the artist, they were broken down in order to understand environments from the perspective that 'the fiction is out there', not imposed by our fantasies. Artists were no longer required to dream, because the world produced its own extreme fictions. Rather, Ballard considered himself and Paolozzi compilers of vast information reservoirs relying on crude means of retrieval, but accessing powerful inventories of the world, awaiting the arrival of more efficient and compelling technological means of accruing more detailed data (the internet and world wide web lay about twenty years in the future). As early as 1971 Ballard said:

"Technology may make it possible to have a continuous feedback to ourselves of information. I think that the biggest need of the painter or writer today is information. I'd love to have a tickertape machine in my study constantly churning out material: abstracts from scientific journals, the latest Hollywood gossip, the passenger list of a 707 that crashed in the Andes, the colour mixes of a new automobile varnish. In fact, Eduardo and I in our different ways are already gathering this kind of information, but we are using the clumsiest possible tools to do it: our own hands and eyes."[13]

Thus the role of collage, which combined text and image, remained a central means of processing the information the world disgorged, in order to track its extremes. The issue of receiving information that increasingly registered a world of renewed conflict with more channels communicating it and reacting to it was more difficult to accommodate. While Paolozzi and Ballard had incorporated the secondary medium of the Vietnam War, film (the primary one was TV), in some of their output,[14] they chose to rely on fairly static ways of representing the war, through printed image and text, albeit in collage form or short story form. Paolozzi's 'novel', *Why We Are In Vietnam* is the most salient example. It is a collection a photographs of black cross-dressers and rounds of ammunition, statistics on student resistance to draft-dodging and pro-Communism, and a collage of 'BAD NEWS AT THE BREAKFAST TABLE' ('Sniper Slays Two, Wounds 11 on Coast Highway; 44 Airliner Death Laid To Passenger Who Shot 2 Pilots; Mad Scientist Shoots 3, Kills Self at A-Lab). Despite these more strident approaches to American culture, for Paolozzi at least the more exposed setting of his public exhibition led to the obscuration of a direct political message, owing to the conflation that lay at the heart of the collage process. In Ballard's case, the subject ironically became a problem owing to the decision of his publishers in the US to choose a particularly incendiary short story title to stand in for his preferred one, **The Atrocity Exhibition**, for its release in North America.

THE TATE AND THE WAR

In 1971 the Tate Gallery, London, exhibited the defining retrospective of Paolozzi, displaying a combination of themes addressing and lampooning the dominance of minimalism in art, staging the Vietnam war as an arsenal of bomb-sculptures, and unveiling the recurrent psycho-sexual allure of consumer culture that Paolozzi and Ballard harnessed in order to create counter-worlds amplifying the encroachment of the modern technological and increasingly corporatized environment on inner states. The eroticisation of technology, fetishisation of the machine, systematisation of the body, and the libidinal flows and blocks that played out across culture and within the life-worlds of modern post-atomic humanity were plain to see, once both artists had jettisoned the more obvious tropes and devices of science-fiction and pop art. The transformation from the early work, of drowned worlds and depopulated beaches for Ballard, and the early pop of Paolozzi's collages, opened out onto a more violent, critical and colder universe of imagery, both visual and literary. Yet the real violence of the war overshadowed them, and impinged on their work.

Ballard was not involved in the Tate show, but the exhibition featured the important screen-prints and montages of the 1950s and 1960s he had collaborated with. Paolozzi himself relegated the sculptures that had made his name in the post-war period to a small room he called the 'chamber of horrors'. In another gallery he presented an arsenal of bombs, alongside reproductions of the two atomic devices that fell on Japan. Referring to Warhol's 'boring' pop art, Paolozzi stated, 'Well, you know the bombs at the Tate are my answer to the Brillo boxes'. Later: 'I don't want to make prints that will help people to escape from the terrible world. I want to remind them.' However, the art critic Guy Brett thought that such objects were opaque repetitions of historical obviousness, stating that 'His recent replica-sculptures of bombs build up this wall of hardware. Of course there is an irony in using such obvious symbols, but surely enough years have been spent under the shadow of the bomb as a monster. We want to see through it.'[15] For Brett, at best Paolozzi's show reverted to a finicky techniques that added fine art touches to the everyday world and thus deviated from a direct engagement with it.

Frank Whitford, who worked on the show and wrote the catalogue introduction, commented on the critical response:

"The exhibition was crucified by the critics. I remember Robert Melville, who was one of the leading critics then, writing in the New Statesman, saying 'There is an exhibition on at the Tate. It is by Eduardo Paolozzi, who used to be a sculptor', full stop. And everything else was a bit more drawn out but as devastating. And I think Eduardo really was quite hurt by this."[16]

Retrospectively, Robin Spencer recognised both Paolozzi's attempt to attack not only the business of fine art but also the industry of war. He noted the complete invisibility of Paolozzi's political art:

"But he accepted philosophically that the art world was effectively controlled by big business and he was ultimately content to have his art improve society rather than transform it. His 1971 exhibition at the Tate Gallery was the most articulate and trenchant protest against the Vietnam War ever made by any artist, American or European; but for reasons not hard to imagine it has been totally expunged from the record of art history."[17]

Paolozzi's attempts to install within his historical oeuvre a present-tense that referred to the stale convictions of art markets as well as a contemporary war only a television picture away seemed to cancel itself out. Received as either a retrospective rumination on atomic war, or a dislocated and inchoate exhibition that collapsed past successes into a current mélange of contradictory messages, the show appeared to fail. This led Paolozzi to abandon his use of war as content, steadily retrieve his standing as an artist of public art, and withdraw to some extent from the British art scene (choosing West Germany as a preferred location). However his use of bricolage would bring about the major success of his exhibition *Lost Magic Kingdoms* (1985-87), shown at the Museum of Mankind, London. By then, the emerging discourses of post-colonialism, renewed artistic interest in ethnology and Paolozzi's attempts to locate his art in the context of other cultures provided a new paradigm into which his way of re-assembling cultures seemed to fit. While the political content was absent, the technique of placing his collection and art in glass cases alongside objects from other cultures hinted at the capacity of his art to appear, as Ballard had once said, as if discovered by some explorer of worlds since vanished. This affirmed what Lawrence Alloway's earlier view that Paolozzi's art appeared as 'clay tablets unearthed in a sunken empire town. Anonymous fingers trace a pattern, unknown, soon to be solved by a Jesuit with a calculating machine'.[18]

Ballard's withdrawal from the war was not as dramatic, for his involvement had stretched only as far as occasional references in interviews and short stories. However, in 1972 Ballard's novel **The Atrocity Exhibition** was published in the US under the title **Love And Napalm: Export USA**:[19] 'I was opposed to using that title. The title is from one of the pieces in that book, but I thought it was a bad title to pick because it sounded anti-American. And it's not about Vietnam... but they insisted'.[20] Ballard had told the publisher that the Vietnam War was over even before it in fact ended, and claimed the man did not want to recognise the fact. Paul Theroux's negative review seized on Ballard's 'observations on "the latent sexual character" of the Vietnam war, which lead him to conclude with the deranged imagining that this war, for Americans, is a form of love.'[21]

As the decade progressed Ballard also began to move away from his association with collage techniques, while continuing to publish short stories and maintain his interest in Surrealist painting. The theme of war gradually receded, replaced with the success of his novel **Crash**, and later the cooler, postmodern vision of achieved dystopias, realised in the air-conditioned villas of Canne's bored corporate classes, or the sterile malls strewn around Surrey and the M4 corridor.

The late 1960s connection of Paolozzi and Ballard culminated in a sharing of techniques and subject-matter, and in certain cases mixed media. However, each then chose to continue mainly within their own field, Ballard in literature, Paolozzi in sculpture and printing. The subject of the war, and of conflict, arose in their work with more or less direct reference to events that cast the USA in an aggressive form quite different to its incarnation in the two artists' love affair with American culture before and during WWII. This change resulted in their eventual departure from exploiting American culture as subject matter in their work. Both, in their own ways, had turned to Europe for inspiration. Ballard's dystopianism meant that subject matter became more important than adventures with process and medium. Paolozzi's conviction in the latter ensured any messages he wanted to send about the state of modern life, its conflicts and contradictions, were buried under his resurgent interest in monumentality, public sculpture and recognition.

Arguably, their relationship cooled towards the end of the 1970s. Ballard remarked on corporate advertising, and the acquisition of the accoutrements by the company world: 'super-executive toys that are bought along with the matching leather furniture, the helicopter and the Paolozzi sculpture in the director's forecourt'.[22] Ballard's connection to the visual world of the Surrealist painters and early visionaries – 'dreams dreamt by sleepers who are awake' – remained a touchstone for his forays into the language of social malady, of collective madness as the final consumer choice.

For both, the historical fact of war receded within their work, to be replaced with new forms of conflict: for Paolozzi a struggle to secure his legacy within the art establishment, and for Ballard a dissection of types of violence expressed in the enmities of the professional classes, and the psychopathy of suburban life: war on the home front.

NOTES

1. *The Glasgow Herald*, December 5 1987, p.11.
2. Designed and carved by Alan Collins in a landscaped garden by Geoffrey Jellicoe, the inscription on the large stone block reads 'This acre of English ground was given to the United States of America by the people of Britain in memory of John F. Kennedy, Born 29 May 1917, President of the United States 1961-63, died by an assassin's hand 22 November 1963'.
3. 'Runnymede, England. An explosive device seriously damaged the memorial to the late President John F. Kennedy at Runnymede Saturday Night. Police have an open mind whether the damage was the work of anti-war demonstrators.' *St. Petersburg Times*, San Francisco, Monday October 8 1968. p.1.
4. In 1977 Ballard returned to the theme, with the story **Theatre Of War**, documenting for TV atrocities inflicted by the US army soldiers on the new peasantry in the UK's future civil war.
5. Robin Spencer, *Eduardo Paolozzi: Writings and Interviews*, Oxford: Oxford University Press, 2000, p.155.
6. Andrea Juno & Vale, interview, in *Re/Search*, No. 8/9, 1984, p.156.
7. J.G. Ballard, 'The Real Empire of the Sun: J.G. Ballard on how his childhood inspired the gripping war film', *Mail Online*, 24 April 2009.
8. Jeanette Baxter, *J.G. Ballard: Surrealist Imagination: Spectacular Authorship*, Farnham; Burlington: Ashgate Press, 2009, p.66.
9. James Pardey, 'David Pelham: the Art of Inner Space', in *Ballardian* Feb 26th, 2012. Pelham adds that it is a 'witty iconoclastic text by Ballard that has been cut and pasted by William Burroughs'.
10. J.G. Ballard, The Art of Fiction No. 85, in *The Paris Review*, Winter 1984, No. 94.
11. See for example 'Nevada Learns to Live with the Atom: While Blasts Teach Civilians and Soldiers Survival in Atomic War, the Sagebrush State Takes the Spectacular Tests in Stride, with 12 Illustrations', *National Geographic*, June 1953, Vol. 103, No. 6. The reverse cover is an advertisement for Coca-Cola, featuring a pin-up girl with a gas pump.
12. SPECULATIVE ILLUSTRATIONS: Eduardo Paolozzi in conversation with J.G. Ballard and Frank Whitford', *Studio International*, 1971, Volume 182, 136–143.
13. ibid.
14. Main examples are Paolozzi and Dennis Postle's animation film *The History Of Nothing* (1962), and Ballard's script and appearance in Harley Cokliss's film **Crash!** (1971), where he borrowed Paolozzi's 1963 book title *Metallisation Of A Dream* to evoke the car as the pre-eminent projected technological fantasy of the 20th century.

15. Guy Brett, 'Paolozzi's Hoard', *The Times* (London, England), Saturday, Sep 25, 1971; p.9.
16. Gilly Booth and Chris Horrocks, *Eduardo Paolozzi: the Artist who Invented Tomorrow*, 'Interview with Frank Whitford', unpublished film documentary interview transcript, 2008.
17. Robin Spencer, *Art International*, 'A Tribute to Eduardo Paolozzi', 15/09/05.
18. Lawrence Alloway, *Metallisation Of A Dream*, 1963.
19. J.G. Ballard, **Love And Napalm: Export USA**, New York: Grove Press, 1972. Preface by William S. Burroughs.
20. Andrea Juno & Vale, interview, in *Re/Search*, No. 8/9, 1984, p.11.
21. Paul Theroux, 'The Auto Crash as Sexual Stimulation', *The New York Times*, October 29, 1972.
22. Andrea Juno & Vale, op. cit., p.27.

THE PSYCHOTIC SCREEN: J.G. BALLARD AND THE MONDO MOVIE

NOTES BY JACK SARGEANT

In the chapter **Tolerances Of The Human Face** in J G Ballard's experimental novel **The Atrocity Exhibition** there is a brief allusion to the film work of Gualtiero Jacopetti: "Zooms for some new Jacopetti, the elegant declensions of serialized violence".[1] In some way this sentence is all that is needed to describe Jacopetti's cinematic masterwork, the documentary *Mondo Cane* (co-directed by Franco Prosperi and Paolo Cavara, 1962). The first of the mondo – or shockumentary – cycle of movies to which it gave its name, *Mondo Cane* can be translated as 'dog world' or 'world gone to the dogs'; however, as a result of both the film and the subsequent genre the word 'mondo' has emerged as a blanket term for anything that may be popularly considered weird, strange or unusual. Jacopetti followed with *Mondo Cane 2* (1963) and *Africa Addio* (aka *Africa Blood And Guts*, 1966, co-directed with Franco Prosperi). Simultaneously the mondo genre spun off titles such as *Mondo Freudo* (Lee Frost, 1966), *Mondo Bizarro* (Lee Frost, 1966) and *Mondo Mod* (Peter Perry, 1967) amongst others, most of which followed the thematic and stylistic framework that was introduced by *Mondo Cane*, although with one notable change; an increasing dependence not on authentic material but on staged footage.

Mondo Cane combined quasi-anthropological film and newsreel footage to create a shifting portrait of the broadly primitive nature of all humanity. Constructed with a dreamlike logic that structured scenes in a manner that appeared as almost arbitrary, the film set the thematic template for much of the genre, and covered topics such as tribes people engaged in rituals, cargo cults, unusual religious ceremonies, strange rites and rituals, exotic foods, the 'weirdness' of modern art, cruelty to animals, animals attacking people and, where possible, hints at sexuality and sex. A narrator links the footage together with darkly humorous and occasionally salacious dialogue delivered in suitably professional tones. *Mondo Cane* finds a brutal exoticism in the world, whether exploring a mass ritual pig slaughter amongst a gathering of tribes or drunken Germans stumbling through the early morning streets, and presents the whole in a gloriously lurid colour palette. Searching for the shocking and the exotic, the film eschewed any overt political message or social commentary, to the chagrin of some critics who were unable to engage with what appeared to be an ambiguous and voyeuristic work. In an essay in *The Atlantic*, Pauline Kael wrote: "audiences that enjoy the shocks and falsifications, the brutal series of titillations of a *Mondo Cane*, one thrill after another, don't care any longer about the conventions of the past, and are too restless and apathetic to pay attention to motivations and complications, cause and effect."[2]

Interviewed by Mark Goodall, J.G. Ballard recalled seeing the film, and others in the genre, in the 1960s at cinemas in central London. For the writer they "were an important key to what was going on in the media landscape of the 1960s, especially after the JFK assassination. Nothing was true, and nothing was untrue".[3] The moral ambiguity of the films and the surreal flow of images and sound gave them the kind of random structure associated with the unconscious mind, or perhaps a visual version of the dissident surrealist journal *Documents* which was edited by Georges Bataille and featuring contributions from the likes of André Masson and Michel Leiris on topics as diverse as abattoirs, angels, modern art, excrement and ethnography.

For Ballard the mondo genre represented the emergent mediascape of the 60s, combining "cunningly mixed genuine film of atrocities, religious cults and 'Believe-it-or-not' examples of human oddity with carefully faked footage".[4] The dreamlike and dissociated nature of *Mondo Cane*'s documentary trajectory and its collapsed narrative can be found echoed within **The Atrocity Exhibition**, which shifts through a series of what the author termed condensed novels. These are micro-epics of media saturation and psychosexual dissonance that are reworked and refigured through various scenarios as the book develops, each aspect a layer in a whole which appeals to discord rather than conventional narrative flow. With its sequences that explore psychosis, the death of modern icons, polymorphic phantasies and fetishism, unfolding throughout the text, the book itself functions in a manner that distinctly recalls the mondo movie.[5] A stream of texts straight from the id and the collective media unconscious that culminate in a luminous image of contemporary psychosis, devoid of any moral certainty: "My fiction really is investigative, exploratory, and comes to no moral conclusions whatever."[6]

NOTES

1. J.G. Ballard, **The Atrocity Exhibition**, London: Fourth Estate, 2006 (1970), p.107.
2. Pauline Kael, 'Are Movies Going to Pieces?' *The Atlantic*, November 1964.
3. Mark Goodall, 'Look Out, It's Real: J.G. Ballard on Mondo Cinema and the 1960s', *Vertigo*, vol 3, issue 9, Spring-Summer, 2008.
4. J.G. Ballard, p.124.
5. There is in fact a mondo-like form of febrile exotica at play throughout J.G. Ballard's literature, from the description of the swamps of post-history in early novels such as **The Drowned World** (1962) through to images of roving bands of feral primitives prowling the silent and darkened corridors and elevator shafts in **High Rise** (1975) and the lonely desert island reworked as a patch of land between motorways in **Concrete Island** (1974). In these visionary books the familiar shifts almost imperceptibly, becoming unfamiliar yet somehow recognizable.
6. J.G. Ballard quoted in Andrea Juno and V Vale, *Re/Search: J.G. Ballard*, no. 8/9, Re/Search Publications, 1984, p.43.

INNER LANDSCAPE: AN INTERVIEW WITH J.G. BALLARD 1970

BY ROBERT LIGHTFOOT AND DAVID PENDLETON

J.G. Ballard is one of a small group of English writers who are gradually transforming the old escapist science-fiction into what is virtually a new literary genre. After the publication of his first novel – **The Drowned World** – Ballard was hailed as 'one of the brightest new stars in postwar fiction'. Subsequent stories revealed the moulding of a new narrative technique and a tremendous gain in the density of ideas and images. In such short stories as **The Assassination Weapon** and **You: Coma: Marilyn Monroe**, the elements of sequential narrative had been almost completely eliminated, and each could be regarded a complete 'novel'. Ballard's complex prose is concerned with the 'inner space' of the unconscious. 'It seems to me that so much of what is going on, on both sides of the retina, makes nonsense unless viewed in these terms. A huge portion of our lives is ignored, merely because it plays no direct part in conscious experience.' (*New Worlds* 1966) His novels merge the 'outer realities' of the 20th century – the atrocities, car crashes, cult figures like James Dean and President Kennedy, the media landscapes – with fragments and images from the psyche. Ballard has also experimented with the advertising of abstract ideas. (A full page ad shows a woman masturbating and bears the text 'Does the angle between two walls have a happy ending? Fiction is a branch of neurology. The scenarios of nerve and blood vessel are the written mythologies of memory and desire. Sex: inner space.') His story in *Ambit* magazine called **Plan For The Assassination Of Jacqueline Kennedy**, led to complaints from the American Embassy; and a recent exhibition of crashed automobiles at the ICA has made Ballard a controversial figure in the straight press.

This interview was conducted some time before the publication of his new novel, **The Atrocity Exhibition**, and took place at his home in Shepperton.

Q: Much of modern literature seems to be a direct reaction against the ideas of the previous literary generation.

BALLARD: I think that the great strength of science fiction is that there is no past – it's all future and it tallies with the way people look on their lives today. I mean look at most people and you will find that they have declared a moratorium on the past; they are just not interested. One is constantly meeting people who have only a hazy idea of their parents – who have changed their life-styles since their childhood in every possible way. In a genuine way they have transformed themselves. It's rather like Los Angeles, where people can adopt any role they like and be convincing in that role. I think this is probably true of Europe as a whole and that it is spreading. When it does there is going to be a stupendous renaissance. I see the year 2000 AD as an incredible one.'

Q: Can even science fiction continue adapting to meet this future? Doesn't all literature eventually reach a point beyond which it cannot progress?

BALLARD: I do not think so. What all writers are trying to do is find the minimum fiction threshold, reducing the volume of fiction within their narratives to a point where a threshold of credibility is reached. Too much fiction and the thing begins to look as unwieldy as a cardboard cake. One has to lower the elements of fiction and screen... find the techniques of dealing with one's subject matter, whether cutting up scientific papers or anything else. Where one eliminates the fictional elements, the number of characters, the events – you try to screen out these elements so that one can make the narrative credible.

Q: How would you view the role of the writer in the next century?

BALLARD: This is something that bothers me all the time because the writer's whole relationship to his subject matter has changed and become totally transformed. A hundred years ago one has the impression that people had made a clear distinction between the outer world of work and of agriculture, commerce and social relationships – which was real – and the inner world of their own minds, day-dreams and hopes. Fiction on the one hand; reality on the other. This reality which surrounded individuals, the writer's role of inventing a fiction that encapsulated various experiences going on in the real world and dramatising them in fictional form, worked. Now the whole situation has been reversed. The exterior landscapes of the seventies are almost entirely fictional ones created by advertising, mass merchandising... politics conducted as advertising. It is very difficult for the writer. Given that external reality is a fiction, the writer's role is almost superfluous. He does not need to invent the fiction because it is already there. So he now has a much more analytic role – you can see this coming in new writers who do cutups with their material. I can visualise the writer – and I have already started doing this – reading scientific journals and taking his fiction ready made from them. Because science is now the greatest producer of fiction and there are thousands of scientific journals produced, particularly the 'soft sciences', the psychological sciences, the social sciences. It is absolutely extraordinary the material they are churning out... look at the psychological abstracts for example.

Q: Why is it that with the opening of so many new horizons in psychology, modern writers still stick to Freud and his ideas, when people like Eysenck seem to suggest that he was misguided, not necessarily in what he said but in his approach?

BALLARD: The great thing about Freud is that from the writer's standpoint it is an extremely useful psychology. Freud sees the unconscious as a narrative stage upon which the whole business of human experience is being dramatised. His psychology is one of dramatics; of dramatic re-enactments. Things like the Oedipus complex are dramatic structures. The whole dynamics of Freudian psychology lend themselves very well to a writer who would find other types very much more difficult to handle. One cannot discount everything Freud said, however. As a metaphor it is true even if it may not be completely true in fact. It works as a metaphor the same way the life of Christ works even if you are not a Christian. Make a distinction therefore between a literal and a metaphorical truth.

Q: You have been quoted as saying that all other forms of literature other than science fiction are doomed to irrelevance. Why dismiss some of the greatest figures in the modern literary tradition like Eliot and Joyce?

BALLARD: I don't dismiss them. They represent the literary culture and tradition that I was brought up on, as we all were. These people created the intellectual landscapes of our minds to a large extent. No, what I was trying to say was that it seemed to me that the so-called 'modern movement', which most people think of as something very contemporary, was in fact the least appropriate intellectual tradition for dealing with 20th century life, particularly the late 20th century, for it is a fiction of introspection, of alienation and so on... it does not seem to me to relate to the needs of today. The future is probably going to be something like Las Vegas for example – this is already coming to a certain extent. Therefore one is going to need... the trouble with Marxism is that it is a social philosophy for the poor. What we need is a social philosophy for the rich. One needs for the year 2000 AD a literary tradition capable of making sense of life as we actually experience it. In the visual arts this has already been done; look at the pop painters who discovered the beauty and importance of the iconography of everyday life, from coca cola bottles to radiator grills. Not just the world of these objects, but also the way in which they interact with our own personalities, our own movements through time and space. They have discovered the importance of the present and have gone completely away from other figurative traditions. The tendency, for example, to put guitars and jugs on tables to formalise objects within the traditional narrative space of painting whatever the particular figurative... (pause)... the pop painters discovered a completely new vocabulary that was really relevant to people, that made sense of people's lives.

Q: While we are on the subject of art, do you see any relationship in your early novels, like **The Drought**, between the visual landscapes of the surrealists and your own literary landscapes?

BALLARD: The classic landscapes of the surrealists like Tanguy, Ernst and Dali confirmed my own hazy views – my own interior landscape. They have always been not a tremendous inspiration, because I would have written the same fiction had I never seen a Dali painting, but reminders that these landscapes extended beyond the borders of my own head. They were valid for a great number of people. It has always seemed to me that science fiction and surrealism have a great deal in common. They both represent the marriage of reason and unreason. In both you have science as sort of quantifying elements. In both science fiction and surrealism the basic source of imagination is one's own mind rather than the external world. Both are the perfect model for dealing with the facts of the 20th century. As for Dali, it seems to me he has created a completely new landscape out of the concepts of Freudian psychology. No other painter that I know of has so well represented the world of the Oedipus complex, of our own childhood anxieties – about memory – always done within the context of the 20th century. In surrealism, the events of the interior world of the psyche are represented in terms of commonplace situations. In fantastic art, Breugel, and Bosch, you have the nightmare represented extremely well... chariots of demons and screaming arch-angels and all the materials of horror... what you don't have is what surrealism has: the representation for the first time of the inner world of the mind in terms of ordinary objects – tables, chairs, telephones.

Q: In science fiction, is an objective state of mind being represented, or is it the subjective state of mind of the writer?

BALLARD: To a large extent one is representing one's own state of mind deliberately, since it is the only reality one knows. We move through a landscape composed of fictions; our own minds, the postures of our bodies, the world of our senses, is the only reality. Given this position, one's own personality becomes the yardstick by which one constructs the architecture of any kind of possibility... within ordinary life or within the novel. So that the word 'subjective' no longer has the pejorative overtones it used to have. Quite the opposite.

Q: Your fiction seems recently to have become preoccupied with the image of the automobile and the car crash.

BALLARD: Well I'm not hung up on automobiles. It is just that it struck me as a metaphor and a key experience that no-one had ever looked at. The attitude to the motor car accident was rather reminiscent of the Victorian attitude to sex in dreams. The people all assumed an attitude to the accident which was altogether different from what they really felt. Take the deaths of people like Jayne Mansfield, James Dean and so on – even Kennedy's death which was a kind of modified automobile accident. The role of the car seemed to be a key to the significance of whatever had happened. It is the most dramatic experience that anyone will ever go through in their whole lives, apart from their own deaths, simply because one is insulated in late 20th century life from real and direct experience. Even sexual experience is muffled by a whole overlay of conceptualisation... fashion, chit-chat and everything else. The car crash is real; it is a violent experience that you are not likely to get in any other area. It is a massive collision of the central nervous system... like a bad trip... a total explosion of the senses.

Q: To turn to your own future: do you intend to explore any new medium... to go into films perhaps, like Dali?

BALLARD: I would like to, but my basic approach is that of a writer. I do not think that the writer is going to be able to rely so much on the materials of his own imagination. As I have said, he has got to adapt and take the materials of his fiction from the world around him; he is going to be more of a commentator than an inventor. The writer cannot compete with the world of media landscapes, inventing fictions at a rate of authority and conviction that no writer can match.

Q: What ideals do you hold as a writer?

BALLARD: I suppose to isolate the truth of any situation as I see it and to try and create in my fiction the moral possibilities of any situation.

Q: Do you see Man as becoming more independent and therefore needing less spiritually?

BALLARD: No, I think that he is merely going to find his sense of the numinous or preternatural in areas very far removed from those in which he found them in the past... in rather unexpected areas. The next religion might come from the world of fashion rather than from any conventional one.

Q: Are you afraid of the future, or do you just accept it?

BALLARD: I am beginning to wonder if the future is going to exist at all. We think – by that I mean science fiction writers – that science fiction enshrines the notion of the future and it takes up its stance vis-a-vis the traditional novel, which is more concerned with the past, and one thinks of past, present and future. But I think that come the year 2000, if not sooner, the past will disappear and the future will go next. People will soon be living only in the present and will not be interested in the future at all. The possibility of maximising our own pleasures, our own intelligent pleasures, will be so great, given the world wide application of computer systems on a domestic level and the enormous possibilities for travel. The present will be so rich, the future will not exist as a possibility. One will be able to lead a completely quantified life; the present will contain its own limitless future. Like... a child going into an amusement arcade does not think 'what will I do and where will I play in five minutes?' He is merely in the flux of alternatives... life is like that.

KRAFFT-EBING VISITS DEALEY PLAZA: A CONVERSATION WITH J.G. BALLARD 1973

BY JEROME TARSHIS

We have had a succession of apocalyptic outrages: the physical universe goes on, but we interpret these events to mean that the moral universe as we thought we knew it has come to an end. The extermination camps of World War II; the bombing of Hiroshima and Nagasaki, and, before that, of Guernica, Ethiopia, Rotterdam, Dresden, Tokyo; the murders of John and Robert Kennedy, of Martin Luther King, Jr., of Malcolm X; the My Lai massacre, the Vietnam war in general; Ulster, the Congo, Biafra, Bangladesh. At a less exalted level, the suicide of Marilyn Monroe and the untimely and ambiguous deaths of Jimi Hendrix and Janis Joplin.

Our mental lives are filled with images of sexuality and violent death presented by the mass media. We may well ask what function these images perform, and whether that function can be separated from the terrible events they describe. Between 1965 and 1969, the British author J. G. Ballard wrote a series of short fictions that explore the meaning of violent images in Western society. Published in various magazines, including *Transatlantic Review, Encounter,* and *Fiction,* they have been collected in a book, **Love And Napalm: Export U.S.A.**, released by Grove Press in 1972.

Love And Napalm is not a masterpiece in the way that, say, *The Great Gatsby* and *Miss Lonelyhearts* are masterpieces, but it is a brilliant and useful book. Like the fictions of Jorge Luis Borges, which it resembles in some of its concerns and in the mock erudition and dryness of its prose, it might well be considered a long poem on metaphysical themes. That is the difficult part; the horrifying part is that this philosophic investigation is conducted in terms of violent death and perverse sexuality.

"In a sense the whole book is about violence," Ballard told me in an interview at his home, near London. "I mean, about violence as a spectator pastime. I see that people's lives these days are saturated with images of violence of every conceivable kind. The strange thing is that although in the past we perceived violence at our nerve endings, in terms of pain and pumping adrenalin, now we perceive violence purely intellectually, purely as an imaginative pastime.

"In Northern Europe, anyway in this country, life is safer than it's ever been before. I think that's probably still true of the United States, notwithstanding the Vietnam war and what is generally described as a very violent society. Compared with South America as a whole, I would say that the United States is a very peaceful country; by and large, the rule of law prevails."

I reminded Ballard that his stories are about the affluent, jaded people one meets in extreme form in Antonioni films, but that those people, and he and I, are part of a very small minority. "Sure," he said. "I write about the landscape in which I live. I can't write about Southeast Asia or South America. But for these people, for this minority, violence is to a great extent an ingredient of their imaginations, a kind of spice which they may need, which may serve some sort of role, and I try to look at the nature of violence.

"Most of us would take the view that violence is wholly bad in all its forms – I would myself – but it may be that certain kinds of violence, particularly those transmitted through the communications media, through television and the news magazines, and so on, have a beneficial role. This is the terrifying irony of an appalling experience like Vietnam – that it may have certain beneficial roles to play. What they are I don't know. I try to offer certain suggestions in the book."

Love And Napalm: Export U.S.A. is made up of fifteen short pieces. In the first nine we find a narrative of sorts about a psychiatrist who is having a nervous breakdown. He is variously named Travers, Travis, Traven, or Tallis – I'll call him Travers – and, although he has a personal history somewhat similar to Ballard's, it is clear that he stands for educated, affluent Western man at this point in time.

Dr. Travers is obsessed by images of death and sex. He cannot accept the aspect of reality that separates us from other persons and things, and our time from other times. Understanding that we now perceive many events solely in the form of sets of images presented to us by some external agency, he begins constructing alternate events. At the beginning of the narrative he is on the staff of "the Institute," a mental hospital near London, and he gives his students the assignment of creating a scenario for World War III, using newsreels, atrocity photographs, and other images. Using the means of conceptual and intermedia art, he tries to re-assassinate John F. Kennedy "in a way that makes sense," to rescue the three astronauts who died in the Apollo capsule, to copulate with Elizabeth Taylor.

Ballard's narrative, reflecting the diversity of the images that make up contemporary consciousness, takes a non-linear form. There is no obvious continuity between one paragraph and the next: some are relatively straightforward descriptions of a physical action; others are listings of objects or images; still others are quotations in which some auxiliary character, speaking for the author, explains the actions of poor, mad Dr. Travers.

We are told of experiments using pictures of sexual acts, war atrocities, genital mutilation. We witness simulated automobile accidents and the violent death, repeated in various forms, of a beautiful young Woman. There are vast billboards of Elizabeth Taylor and Jacqueline Kennedy. The distinction between sanity and insanity, real and imagined events, is not insisted upon; **Love And Napalm** is about violence and sex, but it is also a poetic inquiry into the difference between fictions and realities.

Ballard's mad psychiatrist attempts to build bridges between his unbearably isolated consciousness and the flux of time and events around him. His bridges are made of reproduced images, and for Ballard this points the way toward a future consciousness about which one can feel hope, a consciousness in which anything at all can take on erotic meaning.

Dr. Nathan, one of Ballard's explainers, tells us: "Travers… has composed a series of new sexual perversions, of a wholly conceptual character, in an attempt to surmount the death of affect. In many ways he is the first of the new naives. A Douanier Rousseau of the sexual perversions… At the logic of fashion, such once-popular perversions as paedophilia and sodomy will become derided cliches, as amusing as pottery ducks on suburban walls."

Thus speaks Dr. Nathan. And what does Ballard hope for, if man lives to read the end of the Apocalypse currently in progress? "I think the future of this planet can be summed up in one word: sex. I think sex times the computer equals tomorrow. I think the future of sex is limitless.

"I think the whole of history over the last two or three hundred years has been the harnessing of machines, and of technological systems, to various human activities: to transport, to agriculture, to industry, and so forth. We are getting around to the harnessing of the machine, of computer systems and recording devices, to the sexual impulse. And I think this is absolutely going to transform sex in the way that, say, the jet engine has transformed travel.

"I think the notion of there being any kind of normal sex, that is, heterosexual sex of a genital character, oriented around the reproductive principle, I think that is over and done with now. It might be a phase through which people pass in their early twenties, say, when they get married and have children. But I think it will just be a transient phase in their lives, and they will then move on to their real puberty, a sort of secondary puberty.

"I think largely genital sex will go, too; it will become cerebral sex, where genital sex will playa role – just as dance plays a role in the theater – but will only be a part of the whole. I can see no limits to it whatever. I can see no reason why parents shouldn't have intercourse with their own children, done in terms of love, and in terms of anything else.

"The old fantasies – drinking someone's urine, being beaten by a beautiful woman in black leather – are dead. A new Krafft-Ebing is being written by car crashes, televised violence, modern architecture and design. What we see through the window of the TV set is just as important, sexually, as what the old-fashioned voyeur could see through the window of a bedroom.

"In the future of sex, men and women may not be necessary to one another. Sex might take place between you and an idea, or you and a machine. An incredible range of new unions, new perversions if you will, could be realized by using computer data banks, videotape cassettes, or instant-playback closed-circuit TV. I can see a sexual experience of extraordinary complexity, beauty, tenderness, and love. I can see the magic of sex on a planetary scale, revivifying everything it touches."

But **Love And Napalm** is full of joyless coupling, mutilation, death. "That's not a prophetic book," Ballard said. "I'm trying to describe, as faithfully as I can, the climate as I see it now. I think we're living at a transfer point, where we're moving from one economy of the imagination and the body to a future economy of the imagination and the body. And during this unhappy transfer period it's sadly true that, for all kinds of reasons, people seem to be generating more cruelty than love. I deplore this, but as a writer I've got to face it.

"I think this is the kind of phase individuals go through at times in their lives. An adolescent's first excursions into sexuality tend to be rather fumbled, rather crude, but he will go on. I think we're living at a time when we need, for some reason, an enormous amount of perverse behavior and violence in our psychological diet. They seem to provide some sort of grit which helps us to digest the business of being alive. But they're also stepping stones; they're part of some sort of evolving formula for reaching a better world.

"It's just a fact that we're getting what I describe in *Love And Napalm* as 'the death of affect'; the death of emotion, of any sort of emotional response, is taking place. Let's hope that it gives birth in the future to a new kind of affect; but I think it will be one that will be in partnership with the machine."

After the nine stories that chronicle Dr. Travers' despairing search for new kinds of union, there are six pieces less closely related to one another also concerned with sexuality and violent death. Several of these read like abstracts of the results of market research intended to design a nightmare. Ballard's fiction has always been described as gloomy, and he regrets that nobody seems to notice the irony that runs through the book: he uses the language of behavioral science for ironic effect as Borges uses the language of literary erudition.

In various interviews Ballard has said he is not much of a reader, at least in the sense of keeping up with contemporary writing, and he told me he feels closer to the visual arts than to most modern literature. There is little dialogue in **Love And Napalm**, and the nine sections concerned with Dr. Travers are heavily weighted toward visual description.

The events of the story include exhibitions of paintings and sculpture, conceptual art, and intermedia works. At one point Ed Kienholz's construction "The Back Seat Dodge 38"[1] appears on a road near London. Max Ernst's name is mentioned continually. Dalí, Bellmer, and Tanguy also pop up. Dalí is quoted as having said that mind is a state of landscape, and this idea is one of the keys to understanding Ballard.

"I've always been very interested in the Surrealists," he said, "I think primarily because they're one of the few schools of painting that embrace the imagination without any restraints whatever, but also embrace the imagination within the terms of the scientific language. The Surrealists were interested in optics and all sorts of scientific advances. This climaxed, of course, in psychoanalysis, which was the perfect scientific mythology, if you like, for the investigation of the imagination. And this marriage of science and imagination seemed very close to what I wanted to do as a writer, what I was doing as a writer."

In 1970 Ballard held an exhibition at the New Arts Laboratory, in London, consisting entirely of three crashed cars. "I had an opening party to which I invited a large number of art critics and members of the demimonde. We had closed-circuit television and a topless girl who interviewed everybody in front of the crashed cars so they could see themselves on the TV set. It was a genuine opening, and also an experiment to test one or two of the hypotheses in the book.

"In fact the party was an illustrated episode from the book. What happened was that everybody got extremely drunk incredibly quickly. I've never seen people get drunk so fast. I was certainly within half an hour the only sober person at that gathering. People were breaking the bottles of red wine over the cars, smashing the glasses, grabbing the topless girl and dragging her into the back of one of the cars. Brawls broke out.

"There was something about those crashed cars that tripped off all kinds of latent hostility. Plus people's crazy sexuality was beginning to come out. In a way, it was exactly what I had anticipated in the book without realizing it.

"The show was on for a month. During that time, the cars were regularly attacked by people coming to the gallery. Windows that weren't already broken were smashed in, doors were pulled off, one of the cars was overturned, another car was splashed with white paint. When the exhibition was over, the cars were well and truly wrecked, which I thought was an interesting example of people's real responses to the whole subject of crashed cars."

The relationship between sex and the automobile is the subject of Ballard's most recent book, **Crash**, scheduled to be published by Jonathan Cape in London. For Ballard, the experience of driving an automobile, continually in danger of pain, mutilation, and death, which can be averted only by a series of correct decisions, is a central metaphor, or analogue, of sexuality and of modern life itself.

"As I've said, life is very peaceable, certainly in this country," Ballard told me. "The car crash is the most dramatic experience in most people's lives, apart from their own deaths, and in many cases the two coincide. I think there's something about the automobile crash that taps all kinds of barely recognized impulses in people's minds and imaginations. It's a mistake to adopt a purely rational attitude towards events like the car crash; one can't simply say that this is a meaningless and horrific tragedy. It is that, but it's other things as well, and in **Crash** I've tried to find out what exactly it is."

Ballard considers himself a science fiction writer, but not in the spirit of Isaac Asimov, Arthur C. Clarke, or Robert A. Heinlein. "I think the call signal of Sputnik I in 1957 was the death knell of that kind of science fiction," he said. "To a large extent, the future described by the science fiction writers of the forties and fifties has already become our past."

He believes that the most fruitful area for a mature science fiction – which he considers to be coextensive with a mature fiction – is the intersection between the outer world of physical and technological reality and the inner world of thought and fantasy.

James Graham Ballard was born in Shanghai in 1930. When World War II broke out, he and his family were interned by the Japanese. After the war, he went to England and entered Cambridge to study medicine. Although he never completed his medical studies, the vocabulary stuck: **Love And Napalm** is richly brocaded with anatomic terms, and many characters in his books are physicians.

Ballard had been writing, without attempting to publish, since the age of ten. But in 1951 he entered a short story contest at Cambridge and won it. "That was a green light," he told me. After leaving Cambridge he was variously an RAF pilot, a porter, and a writer of scientific films. He began writing science fiction in 1956 and soon became a fulltime free-lance writer. After publishing a number of stories and novels laid in the future, Ballard set out "to rediscover the present".

"More and more, everything around us is fictional," he said. "That is, it's invented to serve somebody's imaginative ends, whether it's a politician's, or an advertising agent's, or our own. It's particularly prominent in the field of politics, but even an airline flight from, say, London to New York is almost entirely a fictional experience created by advertisers, designers, market researchers. In our time, science, especially so-called behavioral science, is the largest producer of fiction."

We educated readers don't watch the boob tube all day and all night; we don't loiter at the scene of an automobile accident hoping for a glimpse of the victims; we don't wonder how well Ari satisfies Jackie in bed. But we may have been titillated by Konrad Lorenz telling us that competition and aggression are built into the animal, or by Marx telling us they aren't. We buy the visions of new Blakes, with advanced degrees, who find new heavens and hells in studies of Gestalt psychotherapy, extreme experience, the clitoral orgasm, the population explosion, the impending race war.

"The fiction writer's whole role has changed," Ballard said. "The fiction is already there; I feel the writer's job is to put the reality in." Created for the age of Auschwitz, Hiroshima, Dealey Plaza, My Lai, Bangladesh, all brought to us by news magazines or television, J. G. Ballard's surreal landscapes do not show us reality in the form of answers; if we work hard, we can find some brilliantly formulated perplexities.

Two weeks before the publication date of **Love And Napalm: Export U.S.A.** in the United States – under its original title, **The Atrocity Exhibition** – the publisher, Doubleday, which had already printed and bound the book, suddenly withdrew it and destroyed all available copies. The official explanation I have, in a letter from Lawrence P. Ashmead, the editor who bought the book, is that the decision was taken out of his hands; the company's lawyers had decided the book was libelous.

One story in the book had already appeared in *Transatlantic Review*, two in *Encounter,* and others in *Ambit*, a London quarterly, *New Worlds*, a science fiction magazine, and *ICA Eventsheet*, which is published by an art museum. It is true that one story appeared in the underground newspaper *International Times*, but aside from that **Love And Napalm: Export U.S.A.** was put together from tearsheets of the utmost respectability. Ironically enough, Doubleday itself had published two of the offending stories in an anthology in 1968. And there had been no libel suits.

After Doubleday dropped the book, E.P. Dutton took it on. It was scheduled to be published in April, 1971. "They were enthusiastic," Ballard told me. "In fact they first thought of retitling the book "Why I Want To Fuck Ronald Reagan". They were very keen indeed. And there were going to be no problems. But in April – when they were due to publish – my agent got a letter from Dutton with a huge lawyers' report saying they would be very happy to publish the book if I would agree to all the changes. The changes went on for page after page." Dutton's lawyers wanted Ballard to delete three pieces entirely, and all references in the remainder of the book to Ralph Nader, Lyndon and Lady Bird Johnson, and several other celebrities. "They said if I did that they would publish the book. The only problem was there wouldn't be much of a book left. The whole essence of the book is contained in these sexual fantasies about public figures. They are the key to the book, in a sense. I felt I couldn't go along with that, so I said, "Sorry", and there we are now. And I'm looking for someone else.'

After Dutton finally declined to publish the book, Grove Press contracted for its publication and brought it out without any deletions or changes In November, 1972. It had first been published in England, under the title **The Atrocity Exhibition**, by Jonathan Cape in 1970.

NOTES

1. When Edward Kienholz's "The Back Seat Dodge 38" was first exhibited at the Los Angeles County Museum of Art in 1966, it was labeled "revolting, pornographic and blasphemous" by a number of Los Angeles County Supervisors who publicly requested the closing of the exhibition (*L.A. Times*, March 24, 1966).

SELECTED BIBLIOGRAPHY 1966-73

SHORT FICTION

You : Coma : Marilyn Monroe
Ambit 27, Spring 1966
You And Me And The Continuum
Impulse, March 1966
The Assassination Weapon
New Worlds, April 1966
The Atrocity Exhibition
New Worlds, September 1966
The Assassination Of John F Kennedy Considered As A Downhill Motor Race
Ambit 29, Autumn 1966
Plan For The Assassination Of Jacqueline Kennedy
Ambit 31, Spring 1967
The Death Module (later retitled **Notes Towards A Mental Breakdown**)
New Worlds, July 1967
Homage To Claire Churchill
Ambit 32, London, Summer 1967
Does The Angle Between Two Walls Have A Happy Ending?
Ambit 33, Autumn 1967
Why I Want To Fuck Ronald Reagan
Unicorn Bookshop chapbook, 1968
Love And Napalm: Export USA
Circuit 6, June 1968
A Neural Interval
Ambit 36, Summer 1968
The Great American Nude
Ambit 36, Summer 1968
The University Of Death
Transatlantic Review, Summer 1968

The Generations Of America
New Worlds, October 1968
Love: A Print-Out For Claire Churchill
Ambit 37, Fall/Winter 1968-69
The Summer Cannibals
New Worlds, January 1969
Crash!
ICA Eventsheet, 1969
Tolerances Of The Human Face
Encounter, September 1969
Coitus 80
New Worlds, January 1970
Journey Across A Crater
New Worlds, February 1970
Princess Margaret's Face Lift
New Worlds, March 1970
Mae West's Reduction Mammoplasty
Ambit 44, Summer 1970
Placental Insufficiency
Ambit 45, Autumn 1970
Venus Smiles
Ambit 46, Winter 1970
The Side-Effects Of Orthonovin G
Ambit 50, Autumn/Winter 1972-73

NON-FICTION

Terminal Documents
Ambit 27, London, Spring 1966
The Coming Of The Unconscious
New Worlds, July 1966
Notes From Nowhere
New Worlds, October 1966
Salvador Dalí: The Innocent As Paranoid
New Worlds, February 1969

BOOK AND FILM REVIEWS

La Jetée: Academy One
New Worlds, July 1966
Use Your Vagina
New Worlds, June 1969
Alphabets Of Unreason
New Worlds, December 1969

COLLECTIONS

THE ATROCITY EXHIBITION
Cape, July 1970

NOVELS

CRASH
Cape, June 1973